There is no LONG Distance NOW

Very Short Stories

NAOMI SHIHAB NYE

Greenwillow Books

An Imprint of HarperCollinsPublishers

Acknowledgments

Thanks to my first readers, Madison & Michael Nye, and to the inde-
fatigable Virginia Duncan, Barbara Trueson, and Tim Smith. *Herzli-
chen Dank!* to David Weinberger, Julia Tismer, Dr. Ulrich Schreiber,
the Bleibtreu Hotel, Berlin, and the LiteraturRaum project.

"Thud" will appear in *Sudden Flash Youth: 65 Short-Short Stories*, Persea Books, 2011.

There Is No Long Distance Now: Very Short Stories

The text of this book is set in Simoncini Garamond. Book design by Sylvie Le Floc'h

Library of Congress Cataloging-in-Publication Data
Nye, Naomi Shihab.
There is no long distance now : very short stories / by Naomi Shihab Nye.
p. cm.
"Greenwillow Books."
Summary: Forty short stories by an award-winning author and poet.
ISBN 978-0-06-201965-3 (trade bdg.)
1. Children's stories, American. [1. Short stories.] I. Title.
PZ7.N976Th 2011   [Fic]—dc22   2010025559

11 12 13 14 15 CG/RRDB 10 9 8 7 6 5 4 3 2 1
First Edition

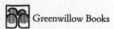 Greenwillow Books

In Loving Memory
Susan Harrison Kaufman

Contents

Introduction

A message arrived. Do you have any short stories 1,000 words or less? I wrote back, No, I do not. Thank you.

A second message arrived. Please send us some of your short stories immediately, 1,000 words or less.

I walked around. I swept the front porch. I sat down and wrote one. It seemed possible.

I wrote some more. Swept the back porch. Leaves and twigs, shells of sunflower seeds. Thank you, birds.

Thank you, minutes and hours and bounties. People walking down the street. Thank you, everything we remember. Distance between thought and action. Distance between suggestion, intention, reality. There used to be a very big difference between local calls and long-distance calls, but now, usually, there is not.

Thank you, lives we did not lead, might like to lead, might still lead.

About a year later, after I turned in some of the revised stories to my real editor Virginia, the man who walks the pitiful fluff-ball dog spoke to me for the first time ever. He said, Did you hear the weather report? It is going to get *very cold*!!!! He said this with great excitement.

The dog was leading him, he was not leading it.

I stuttered, responding. What would he think if he knew he was in a story?

He and his dog are two of the only real characters in this book. So is the taxi driver in Chicago. And the people he mentions.

The other people are all made up.

Really.

Stay True Hotel

Jane's father announced their moves as if they were dinner menus. Pasta with mushrooms. Now, Berlin.

He had a better offer (always) from a fine company. Transferring from her London school into a school in Germany would be no problem. (He would probably feel contented for a year before he got restless again.)

You will like Berlin, I promise, he said.

He had also said this about Dublin, London.

Berlin was spacious, expansive—air cleanly cold in winter, clear in summer. Students rode free on subways, buses. Studied English. Summer light lasted so long a day felt double-wide. Lots of art and music, he said. Everything you love. I promise.

Jane said, You always promise.

🕊

Maybe when your mother died young, you became instantly old. A double-wide child, mother and baby mixed together.

Your mother loved Berlin, he said. Her favorite city.

What?

Sometimes Jane resented her father's guarded style. Why didn't you tell me before?

He stared out the window at the trees they were saying good-bye to.

We weren't there. What good would it have done?

In the airplane Jane watched her father drinking a German beer and eating chips. He didn't look that old, really. A bit handsome, with his messy dark mop, sad eyes. She thought, It is not his fault she died. Maybe he thinks he can leave his sadness behind him and that is why we keep moving.

Germany felt bright, awake. Green fields, silver windmills. The apartment in Berlin would be ready in a month. Till then Jane and her father were moving into a hotel called Bleibtreu. We will navigate the city, her father said. Discreet, gray façade, Bleibtreustrasse Number 31.

While her father did paperwork at the desk, she looked around.

There didn't seem to be a door. Three passageways, a bar, a deli, shop selling antique roses, courtyard with long blue tiled table surrounded by a moat of glittering blue chips. Two metal dog sculptures, one sitting in a cement chair.

Where was she?

On the wall, hearts with words, *Stay True*. White chair sculpture with lights under feet. Glass art, painted plates.

Daddy? she said, which she rarely said. How did you find this place?

Grinning. He had navigated.

They rode excitedly up the glass elevator to Three. Two low white beds, soft cotton sheeting, puffy comforters. Mysterious wooden ladders on the walls next to the beds. Jane unpacked immediately. Placed her favorite picture of her mother on a rung—face turned up, as if to breeze or gentle rain. She turned the handles of the wooden windows, pulled them open.

Across the street, a man watered geraniums on a balcony.

Her father said, Do you want to go with me to check in at the office?

She shook her head.

Okay, feel free, go out, look around.

Jane always felt free. Didn't she?

She ran down the stairs, circled the block. Then three, collecting details for return. Windows lined with checkered shirts, burgundy peonies in buckets. And what was this large pink pipe supported by purple poles?

Ponytailed women in dressy clothes and high heels riding bicycles, miniature dogs in their baskets. Couples gripping hands. Tattoos, canes, studded purses, prams, clicking and humming of the planet. Something snazzy in the pace here.

Jane stared at a street sign, Kurfürstendamm, wondering, Will a name that long ever feel familiar in my head? Sometimes it felt thrilling to be surrounded by someone else's language. Wrapping *"bitte"* and *"danke"* around her tongue felt hopeful. *"Handgebügelt"* scrawled in a window; pastry shop, frilled cakes; Deutsche Post. Stationery stores made her happy. Her father had slipped her twenty Euros— she bought a notebook, blue paper, envelopes, a fistful of thick German pencils with nice dots on them, a wooden sharpener. . . .

By the time she'd rounded many blocks, not even counting anymore, a hunger for absorption overtook her, warm waves on a beach, desire for colors and sounds. How long since she had felt this? A couple approached, pointing at a map, speaking slow English, as if they thought she were German. Though she had arrived only hours before, she could answer. Kurfürstendamm! Pointed, and they smiled—Americans. She never let on that she spoke English.

She stepped back into the hotel, sharpened, stirred. Eyes more vivid. Rocklike handles on cupboards. Deep white-tiled soaking tub. Could she be happy here?

Stay true. True to her Scottish accent? Her mother's smile that never left her? The green rims of land where they used to walk?

She thought, This beautiful city Berlin never wanted to be rubble. Before the war, proud of its boulevards, leafy parks, bustling trains—this city never wished to be struck by bombs, ruined, none of it.

And look at it now. Restored.

Her father had not wanted to be a widower.

Most importantly, her mother had not wanted to die.

But when something happened that you did not want . . . later there might be a long avenue with a German name stuck to it. Ways you could turn.

Jane stared out the window. The watering man was gone now.

Sometimes after long sadness, you needed a new thought. Hold it awhile. Stay true to it. She thought, If I am true to my mother, what do I do? Lift my face up, as she did in this picture? Would she prefer I remain true to gloom?

Jane closed her eyes. A life could change in ten minutes. Then she stepped back toward the hallway, the quiet elevator, rode it down to blue stones in the moat and the colorful chairs placed at angles around the table, and thought, I'll sit here a while. Watch people. There's a man drinking a ginger ale with an orange slice in it.

Already I could write a letter, and I haven't been here a day yet.

When my dad comes back, I'll see a different dad.

Thud

There are many things Rainey does not understand: war, and running with the bulls, for two examples. Why get anywhere near herds of bulls and irritate them in the first place? Why is this popular? She would prefer to be liked by bulls—to meet them in a placid zone and stare at one another.

She has no desire to binge drink or congregate with believers. The pious confidence of people who think they know "the truth" repels her. If only one could slap them with mysteries. . . .

She pictures herself on the edge of any scene. Scenes need fringe observers—people to take notes and tell what you did later.

If you can find them.

Rainey decided to be invisible in her last year of high school.

The episodes seemed so tiresome—who liked whom, who had broken up, or overdosed—flickering hordes of rumors—she abandoned them all. A wide swath of her brain felt relieved. She had no interest in Adderall. She made up a boyfriend named Leo who lived in Wisconsin, where no one she knew had been. His parents were professors who stayed home by the fireplace reading all winter long.

At school if someone asked her to do something sociable, she'd say, "I'm okay." If pressed, she'd say something about Leo. They were working on a long-distance project. Something, anything.

On weekends Rainey pitched a book and water bottle into her basket and rode her bicycle around the abandoned brewery and the ancient mill. One day the waterwheel was spinning again. She watched parents prepare birthday parties for their kids at Roosevelt Park, hanging piñatas, weighting paper tablecloths down with horrible giant soda bottles. She conversed with abandoned dogs and dreamed of delivering them all to the Utopia Animal Sanctuary, where they would be cared for with kindness and attention.

Rainey felt she needed to examine the mysteries of her childhood more deeply before going off to college. Those strange reverberations around the sixth grade year, what was that about? That sense of precipice—as if you'd gone hiking and reached a cliff at the end of the trail and where was your parachute? Because the days were definitely, definitely going to push you off. And if you hadn't learned rock climbing by then, or discovered some way to bungee jump, you were in big trouble. Rainey had never yet fully reckoned with the sixth grade. Was she still standing there, immobilized? Had everyone jumped but her?

This was not something you could talk about with the homecoming queen.

Mostly, she was still pondering the shock of her father's death, when she was a freshman and he was still a relatively young man who had a heart attack after work one day. Strangers called 911 when they saw him slumped against his car in the bank parking lot. He'd been taken to the hospital, and was "well on the road to recovery," said the doctor to Rainey's mother a few days later, the day he died.

Rainey had taken a bus to the hospital right after school, carrying a small tub of tabbouleh, her father's favorite salad. She had a frozen blue ice pack in the pocket of her schoolbag and a plastic spoon. Outside her father's room, she was stunned to be hugged hard by a woman she'd never seen before. A black nurse with an open face wearing a print smock—small yellow bears holding balloons. Who was she?

"He didn't make it, honey. Oh honey, he's just left us," the nurse had stifled a sob.

Was she selected for her softness, her resonant voice?

The official hugger-nurse who stood outside stricken rooms to greet the first people who showed up, alert them they were at a new cliff— surely that must be a weird position to apply for. Professional hard-times hugger.

Rainey wondered some days, if she went to the hospital again, could she find the woman? Could she ask more questions—like, did he call out when he died, did someone hear him? Or was it simply the monitor which began moaning its loud alert? What exactly happened? I'm ready to hear it now, please. Could she tell her, He'll never leave me, just wanted to let you know?

Both Rainey and her mother felt guilty they had not been at his bedside when he died. Rainey's mother had been back at work—she thought he was stable, soon to be released. Apparently people commonly died when their loved ones were out of the room. Bathroom break. Quick trip down to the cafeteria for a grilled cheese. It was easier to die if you didn't have family members to worry about at that exact moment.

Easier for the one who was dying, maybe.

Rainey kept wondering what she would have done had she been there, with her dad. Who expected anyone to have a second heart attack on top of a first? She would not eat tabbouleh again till she was twenty-three.

Did his sudden departure have anything to do with her

inability to negotiate the social roller coaster now?

Then a bird flew into the window of English Literature during a discussion of Gerard Manley Hopkins. Someone tittered. After class Rainey went outside. A gray mourning dove, stunned on the ground. Rainey filled the cap of her water bottle and poured water over the bird's beak. The beak opened a tiny bit. The bird opened an eye.

A boy knelt down beside her. "Hey," he said. "Sad bird. I'm Leo."

Beet Cake

After learning they were both getting B's in their first semester of Culinary Arts, Brin slammed her locker door and Sandi cried in the bathroom stall. They had never skipped class. They adored stirring, chopping, combining ingredients. Weren't they the ones, after all, who had wowed the class with zucchini and thyme omelets and used fresh beets in a cake?

Somehow they had grown giggly during the Garnishing Unit, then fallen behind with Meats.

Sandi said parsley was boring and everyone laughed. She didn't care if it was traditional. She preferred mint or snipped rosemary. Arugula was her fave. Also those loopy red and yellow sauces swirled around desserts—you could paint a plate to look like nursery school.

Brin adored cilantro. She baked an eggplant in the

microwave without piercing it enough and it exploded. But she concocted savory lentils with goat cheese. She and Sandi rolled filo surprises, tucked fancy mushrooms inside, and rolled crusts for small latticed cherry pies when their class-mates chose the easier road, pecan.

Ms. Rippo said they talked too much, staring sternly into her grade book, preferring bland dumplings to cheery paprika girls with pierced eyebrows and pocket chains. Try to focus, please. You've been drifting. She looked up at them, looked past them, and sighed.

Drifting? Sure, they chattered. But talk meant happy, and weren't cooks better off happy?

The next day they felt better. Sandi whispered, "Did you know Irma Rombauer who wrote *The Joy of Cooking* had a horrible life?"

"What do you mean?"

"Her baby died, her husband had nervous breakdowns, and finally killed himself with a shotgun. And then she baked."

"I guess there's hope for us."

"Shhhhh! That's bad."

"Man, I'd like to write a best-seller cookbook and beat it out of here."

They'd watched *Julie and Julia* three times, even though they hated the duck segments.

Sandi said, "We are going to work in vegetarian restaurants."

Brin said, "The cow is still crying in every slab of beef."

Ms. Rippo didn't appreciate their refusal to cook meat.

To make up for it, they focused on the salad unit twice. They had to do more with appetizers. In fact, they had to feed the whole administration on talent show night, practically singlehandedly, as everyone else pretended to be performing. Billy Martin had stolen their tongs and kept denying it. They worried about the cheese, which smelled funny. "Cheese always smells funny," Brin insisted.

Sometimes they got the giggles the minute they tied their white aprons on. A few students had started a rumor they were a lesbian couple. It didn't bother them—they were feeding that, too. They stood with their arms around each other when the principal walked through.

As a freshman, Sandi had played percussion and been kicked out of band for crashing cymbals arbitrarily and making her band mates lose their rhythm on the marching field. Brin had volunteered as a school stagehand, which she enjoyed, but the repetition of rehearsals seemed excruciatingly dull.

At least, with culinary arts degrees, they could someday get jobs. Next year they were hoping to work at the Westin Hotel where NBA stars stayed. They told people they were *going* to work there, as if they'd already been hired. They'd gone down to the Westin for breakfast a few Saturdays, so they could offer helpful suggestions about the buffet when they finally applied.

"*Far* too much emphasis on bacon and sausage. Add more creative grits and potato dishes, more smoky chipotle flavor to the hot sauce, a little picante flair to the huevos rancheros, hello!"

During Christmas break they volunteered at the food bank, prepping and cooking with prisoners from the county jail. Sandi really liked one skinny movie star–looking guy named Rafael, who whispered to her "Don't do dope" as they were scrubbing cookie sheets. He said he dreamed of running a fresh muffin bakery someday, down by the river. The muffins at the jail came out of cellophane. Sandi was impressed they *had* muffins at the jail. She thought they might have only crackers, or dry toast.

Sandi and Brin had tried to talk the food bank into letting them make luscious beet cake with green icing for Christmas, but the food bank said Red Velvet hadn't gone over very well at Valentine's Day, so they'd stick with vanilla and chocolate.

On their first day back after holiday, Sandi said, "Let's visit Ms. Rippo after school, to see if there is extra credit we can start doing right now. Because if we get B's for the whole year, I don't think the Westin will hire us. Come with me?"

Ms. Rippo seemed reluctant to see them when they barged into the cooking lab after the bell. They hadn't made an appointment. She looked at her watch. Brin called her on it, saying, "Oh, don't I have to be somewhere else, girls? Just kidding!" Sandi poked her.

Ms. Rippo coughed.

"You girls need to make a big change," she said. "I actually wish you could have personality transplants. Some days I think, I can't stand to come to school and see those two again! It seems as if you're always making fun of me—everything is an inside joke to you. Do you know how that feels to a teacher? In fact, I don't want to have this conversation right now, unless the counselor is present. I'm afraid of what I might say."

They looked at each other, stunned.

"Afraid?" Sandi gulped. "You mean, you want to say more? We're really that bad?"

Ms. Rippo was crying.

Brin said, "We're so sorry, we'll try to be better! We didn't know we were *that* bad, did we?" She looked at Sandi.

Sandi started crying, too.

"Unbelievable!" Brin said, outside in the blinding light. "Personality transplants? Was that mean or what? I'm in shock!"

Sandi was still crying.

They walked to Brin's house in silence and drank two beers.

Curb

The Christian School has a team called the Warriors—WEL-
COME BACK WARRIORS! shouts the banner over the road.

But the billboard in front of the school says the "Trait
for the Week" is peace.

Victor feels alarmed about entering such a facility.

He may come out confused.

He may emerge wearing a black armband, carrying a
spear.

Why did his friends choose to gather here for their
trash-pick-up organizational meeting? Why didn't they rally
in the drainage ditch?

Victor is excited about his new devotion to picking up
trash. A spear would be helpful, actually. So far his tool
kit includes heavy-duty black garbage bags and a box of

throwaway gloves. He likes the way he looks at the world when he is on duty. Life seems more manageable. No, he can't solve global warming, emission overload, cancer. Yes, he can make sure the Frito bags from last night's cheerleading rally in the parking lot are removed.

Victor attends the public school down the street. But his best friend Bear attends the Christian School. All summer they have been cooperating on a collaborative research project on capital punishment which they plan to present as a senior project at both schools. Their state of Texas leads the nation in killing prisoners. Victor thinks this is one of the many things that gives their state and country a bad reputation—to be lining up with Iran, Saudi Arabia, Iraq, and China, all of whom employ the death penalty. Even Mexico, with its wild drug-smuggling gangs and frequent beheadings, doesn't allow the death penalty.

"See?" Bear always says. "Maybe they need it."

Bear thinks capital punishment is a necessary evil and the justice system is doing a great job. He doesn't worry about all the guns floating around just under the surface of the city, something Victor worries about all the time.

Newspaper mug shots haunt him. Victims, as well as the accused. How many prisoners have wrongfully been killed? Some who might be innocent languish in solitary confinement for decades. The Texas death row facility is ironically located in a town called Livingston. Victor reads ethics papers prepared by University of Texas law professors. Bear reads the Bible. Eye for an eye. Victor asks, Will your father sacrifice your brother if God tells him to? Bear just stares at him.

Victor picks up Popsicle sticks and skinny straw wrappers. Secretly he likes the word "rubbish" more than "garbage" or "trash"—someday he will live in Scotland. This is the first clue.

There is so much trash. How can a city dump be big enough to accommodate the refuse for a million and a half people?

Victor's own sister creates enough rubbish to fill an acre every other day. He read about pneumatic trash tubes in Sweden that suck rubbish for miles underground, to proper recycling facilities. Wide-mouthed tubes stand, four in a row, on the roof of an apartment building. Paper goes in one, plastic . . . a giant sucking sound. He would like to see these tubes.

Victor, Bear, Rudolf, and Angus congregate at a cafeteria table. It turns out that girls are not as interested in picking up trash as Bear hoped they would be. The boys have mapped out their neighborhood; they will each be responsible for certain blocks. Should the project have a name? "Clean Sweep," says Angus. But Victor thinks that sounds

military and fake. Like Desert Everything. Rudolf wants
them to be called Neatniks. *Beatnik* is a word that fell out of
fashion so long ago; they can bring it back with a twist, rein-
vent the concept. Look cool and distant while picking up
trash. They can wear hats. Rudolf thinks attention to trash
will help him get into a better college. He'd love to go to
Yale but it's so far away, expensive, and he's not that smart—
but it's such a neat-sounding name. So brief.

"Do Christians sin more?" asks Victor. "Because they
think they will be forgiven? Has anyone done a study about
how many people on death row were raised Christian?"

Bear says, "I think it's insulting for you to talk this way
in our cafeteria."

"I would like newspaper coverage," says Angus. "The
newspaper always talks about cleaning up the river. But let's
tell them we're focusing on streets and see if they care."

After fiesta parades, embarrassing to say, the streets
became utter wastelands of garbage, baby diapers, shame-
less cluttered filth. How could people do that?

Nothing, nothing, can be taken for granted, Victor is
thinking as he trips off the curb outside the school after
the meeting. He catches himself before falling. It's a much
higher curb than the one at his school. Any of them could
have a disaster before the school year is over. You could
have a disaster an hour from now. Bending over. Something

could hit you. People carry guns in glove compartments and lunch boxes. Cars spin out of control in minor drizzle. The more you know, really, the more you have to worry and fret about. It's a miracle anyone can sleep at all.

He leans over for a gum wrapper. Has to tug on it. It's stuck to the street. He sticks it into his pocket distractedly— no glove, nothing. In the washing machine, the wrapper will adhere to the white collar of his sister's favorite shirt.

Once Victor found a love letter with certain words— *darling, kiss*—crossed out. He smoothed and saved it. Someone else had more trouble writing than he did. He used to think you could put bits of trash together—a man scanning the classified section for an auto mechanics job dropped a plastic bag while unwrapping Juicy Fruit gum and popped his button—to make a story. That was when he still believed.

Somebody Needs
To Be Punished

They were asked, as part of the application, to list five ways they had been punished in their own lives, and five ways they would like to punish, with the option of saying specifically whom and for what.

1. The cloakroom was easy. *You will stand in the back corner of the cloakroom* (even in first grade Lula had lived way beyond the era of cloaks, but no one called it the coat room—it was an ancient school and everything in it was ancient) *with your nose pointing toward a metal hook. You will think, for ten or twenty minutes, about what you did to get sent there. Broke John's pencil point. Broke John's nose.* Or, you could think about cloaks—who wore them, how debonair those lost people felt stepping into their coaches.

When allowed to return to the class, your feelings of humility and lonesomeness will render you a much finer student and person.

2. *You will be sent home.* Lula loved being sent home. Her favorite books were there. She didn't have to go to math. *You will miss your homework assignment. It will be a blot on your record.*

3. *Your father will be sad forever.* His family was booted from their home. Their trees were cut. Their money and dignity was taken. They became second-class citizens—this was not their fault. Refugees had reason to be sad. But it was also a punishment rendered by an occupying force on the future children of the refugees as well as the refugees themselves. Even in another country far away—the children of the refugees, trying always to make their parents happy, never quite succeeding. *But wasn't that a good movie? Didn't you like that drive into the country? Wouldn't you like to have a nice little cup of tea?*

4. *We won't speak to you. And we won't tell you why.* Punishment by silence became strangely popular in the twenty-first century. Sisters and brothers clammed up. They wouldn't talk to you even if you went to their bedroom doors

and said, Hey, I'm really sorry. For what, I'm not sure, but sorry indeed. Doors stayed shut. Countries punished one another by denying talk. Old friends moved away, wouldn't return calls. How could the era of chatter-chatter, texty-text, also be the era of silence? It was like stepping into a jungle where insects buzzed around your face and legs, but above you, the trees weren't giving away anything. Sometimes you could feel the voices of the nineteenth century (reading old poetry, for example) as more fluent and responsive than the voices of the twenty-first. Did I lose your pen? Stain your shirt? Insult your intelligence? The thing about being punished by silence—you thought about it a lot. It haunted you, and grew. What could I have done to make this person so mad at me? They're stupid not to tell me, but still. It was a ballooning kind of punishment.

5. *Remembering your mistakes more acutely than any minor successes.* This was the worst. The things that kept you up at night. Tip to a waiter that was too small. The words that didn't fit the moment. Words that didn't come till too late. You could kill yourself in increments, punishing your spirit day after day—regret. Guilt. Not the guilt of the little girl who woke in the night embarrassed God was mad at her because she had tucked balls under her shirt, pretending to have breasts. "I even felt sexy." That was sweet, and pure,

no crime at all. But the crime of obsessive replay—get rid of it, get rid of it. Who could ever have known the hardest punishments would be the ones you gave yourself?

As for how Lula would like to punish others—she had to chew on her pencil fourteen minutes for this one. It was much harder. She would like to muzzle the crazy dog next door. She would like to drug him. Mellow him out.

2. She would like to appear at the front doors of the ones who were punishing her with silence and throw buckets of water on their heads.

3. She would take away all the weapons. From everyone. Dissolve them. No guns in America, no nukes in Israel, no bad chemicals, no water boards, no missiles, etc. But was this a punishment or a gift? People were just going to have to talk, that was it. That was their punishment. Thank me later.

4. The prisoners already in jail being punished had to learn organic farming and feed all the homeless and there could be no two ways about it. They had to dig and hoe and weed and water and harvest and they even had to cook the food and serve up the plates. Many skills would

be learned this way. Legendary chefs born. People no longer hungry. And ex-prisoners, too occupied to commit
further crimes.

    5. Lula was keeping this one secret. She knew she would
need more punishment for something down the line, but she
wanted to be able to punish herself discreetly instead, when
the time was right—such as, you will extract yourself from
this happy crowd and stare at the orange line of sunset without saying good-bye to anyone, feeling how the night falls
over you, gently, more gently than anyone, with all the flaws
and errors buzzing in our cells, really deserves.

Downhill

Sarah's dad was dialing the phone, calling his brother, who lived in Montana, went fishing night and day, and almost never spoke to anyone.

"Randy, it's time you got your butt down here. High time. We need your help with Mom. It's getting dangerous. She could burn that place down." (Pause)

"Yeah, you heard me right. I don't care what you're doing. The fish will wait. I can't leave my work right now, and Sarah's in school and Melody—well, you know she and Mom never got along. When can you come?"

He got off the phone. In his gruff mood now.

"He won't come."

Sarah said, "It doesn't matter. He's not very nice anyway. Let me just move over there to Granny's and live with her for a month, till she feels better. It's fine."

"But you have to go to school." Her dad knew his mom would probably never feel better. She'd been going downhill for the last ten years. Nothing in particular, just the general decline—eyes, teeth, knees, all of the above. Now she was leaving candles lit on her dinner table for hours after dinner, scary stuff.

"Well, she lives closer to the school than we do. Being with her before and after school is better than no one else being there at all. If she panics at night again, I'll go into her room and talk to her. She has that bell she likes to ring. "

Granny lived on Army Boulevard, an odd street of shabby mansions obscured by tangled armies of vines and giant trees, heaped leaves, secret elders tucked behind closed curtains and blinds.

"It will be fine," Sarah said. "I'll ride the Broadway bus to school. My adventure."

So she packed her suitcase and a plastic tub of books. Tucked in her Aveda shampoo and Kiehl's face cream, the two luxuries of her personal toilette. Her mom, Melody, cried when she departed. "It's like you're already leaving for college," she mourned.

"Well, come visit me," Sarah said. "I'll be studying pill bottles and the *Financial Times*." (Her grandmother subscribed to the *Financial Times* mostly because it was

pink. But Sarah had discovered that the hefty weekend editions, printing more about world culture than
finance, were terrific.) "Bring me some home cooking
now and then."

This was a family joke. Melody didn't cook. Melody got
takeout or made sandwiches.

This was only one of the ten or twenty things her granny
disliked about her mother.

No cooking, no sewing, no ironing, none of the old
domestic skills in sight . . . not even a hemming capability.
Melody took their clothes to Nimble Hands Tailors. She let
the cleaners press her husband's shirts.

That night, Sarah and her grandma ate homemade corn
bread and pinto beans and lit the lamps (this was a phrase
her grandma favored, as opposed to "turning on the small
lights on little tables")—then they puttered around together
in their pastel floral nighties. Sarah thought her month
might feel like a holiday after all. The phone rang. Old land
line with circular dial. Sarah answered, and Uncle Randy
said, "What are *you* doing there?"

"Fishing," she said. A silence. Then she added, "Fishing
in time."

Granny curled in a corner of the brocaded vintage
couch and tucked her feet up. She giggled like a schoolgirl.
She said, "Oh honey!" She said, "Randy, no!"

Sarah eavesdropped on her grandma's side of the conversation from the hallway.

She had never heard her granny laugh like that when speaking to her father. Her father, filled with admonitions and concerns. "Are you taking your medicine? Are you double-locking that front door?"

Randy, on the other hand, seemed to be talking about a tattooed woman he'd met at a biker bar—the woman had her hair in a French braid like Granny used to wear when she was young and he complimented it and they ended up having a date or god knows what. Granny repeated what he said, then added comments. "But tattoos! Honey, I never!"

Long silence. "Ha! Ha! Ha!"

Sarah went into the guest bedroom and looked around. White lace curtains, a crocheted white coverlet neatly tucked. Family lore held that Randy, who'd never finished college, but run off to work on some oil rig by Point Barrow, Alaska, and go salmon fishing on weekends, was the secret genius of the family and Sarah's lawyer dad, a bit of a dullard. This was what Melody told Sarah, anyway, about her own husband.

"Don't say that, Mom," Sarah protested.

"I'm just reporting what I hear," her mom had said. But who did she hear it from?

They spoke for *one solid hour*.

Granny was shouting into the telephone now, "I love you, too, cupcake!"

Randy? Cupcake? He never shaved. He wore smoky-smelling lumberjack checkered shirts and clunky woodsmen boots. He had never married yet and he was—what? Forty-eight?

The world was full of mysteries.

Her granny savored clinky glasses of gin and tonic with dinner.

Would Sarah tell her dad? He said Granny wasn't supposed to have any alcohol with her medicine, but how much fun was Granny having these days and what did it matter? If she died on a Tuesday instead of a Friday, I mean really?

Sarah stepped back into the living room. "That sounded delightful," she said. "What's Uncle Randy up to?"

"Well, you just won't believe it," Granny said. "He is the smartest boy. I mean, a little nutty, but so smart. When he heard about my last panic attack, he decided to start telling me the stories he remembers your grandpa and me telling him when he was little, and tonight he told about the raccoon who lives in a cavernous tree and irons for the other animals. Lovely! I know your dad thinks he's shirked his family responsibilities by living so far north, but he's been my hero all these years."

Easter Bonnet

It was so stupid, really. And it was promoted—by history, culture, groceries, storybooks. The really important stories were buried—what happened to the Indians, for example. And the stupid stories stuck around for generations: a rabbit carrying eggs. Where did he get them, by the way? And where did he live the rest of the time? No convenient North Pole for this guy. Children searching for eggs in damp grass. Eggs packed with quarters and candy.

Sylvia grew up mad at the Easter bunny. She never got a wicker basket piled with plastics and sugars and trans fats like everyone else did.

She never got a pink necklace with little bunny hearts dangling down from it. The bunny shunned her. Her mother wouldn't follow the script.

"This has nothing to do with Jesus Christ as far as I can see. Can you picture it? Jesus Christ carrying an Easter basket?"

Well, who cared? Theo, the boy down the street, whose parents were Southern Baptists, got an Easter basket. Jamie, the adorable redheaded kid at the corner, got an Easter basket. Margaret and her many brothers and sisters, all Catholics, got Easter baskets. Sylvia's mother went to the Church of the Everlasting Arms on the south side of town under the freeway. Sylvia had been dragged there for years, especially since her father ran away to Mexico with the lettuce lady. The minister talked more about blood than eggs. He never talked about rabbits.

One Easter Sunday, Sylvia took notes in church and the minister asked to see her afterward. He wanted to know what she had written on the program. She refused to show him. His sermon had been all about rising up, from the grave, from the cave, from the darkness of despair, from the ashes. Sylvia had written in the margin: Well, they didn't burn Jesus, did they?

The minister seemed suspicious. Sylvia said, "I like to think about things later."

In the car on the way home, passing the men who sold tiny palm trees out of trucks and taco cafes packed with cars for special Easter taco breakfasts, Sylvia's mom said, "What did he want with you? Reverend Ruiz? I saw him talking to you?"

"He liked my haircut," Sylvia said.

For the first time in a while, her mom brought up the lettuce lady.

"Sometimes I think about how your father made fun of her, but it was just a cover-up."

The lettuce lady grew lettuce in her front yard, not her back. The whole little plot furrowed with rows; dark green, light frilly lettuce, arugula, spinach, many tones and sizes of layered leaves. Her house needed painting and her porch chairs had weathered to rust, but her lettuce, abundant. And she was always giving it to everybody. She wore a halter top featuring impressive tanned cleavage. Sylvia's unspoken questions would remain— was her dad really that mesmerized by big boobs? And, wasn't the lady sad about her carefully tended garden withering after she left?

When Sylvia's father ran away with her, in fact, the refrigerator at their own house was packed with about six bags of aging lettuce in various degrees of withering—Sylvia's mom said too much salad gave her diarrhea so she didn't use it all up and Sylvia was, well, a kid. The first thing she made when she got hungry wasn't a salad. Try peanut butter and jelly. Try cheese.

Sylvia's mother was so disgusted with the whole sce-
nario she threw each sack of lettuce down the toilet. Not
in the trash. Bad call. Their plumbing backed up and they
had to get Joey to come fix it and he charged them eighty
dollars to unplug everything, so it was what Sylvia's grand-
father, who also didn't like lettuce, called "insult upon
injury." That was another thing Sylvia wrote down.

"Everything is a cover-up," Sylvia said now, on Easter,
once again frustrated because she would get nothing pretty,
nothing shiny, nothing sweet. "Life is a cover-up."

Her mother looked at her. Her mother drove with both
hands on the steering wheel, like an idiot.

"Don't you talk like that, Missy Prettycakes."

But Sylvia continued. She wasn't afraid of her mother.

"Life is a cover-up for deadness. Jesus is a cover-up for
people who want to sin and get away with it by saying sorry
later. Easter is a cover-up for gluttony. All holidays are cover-
ups for boringness." She could really roll.

"I'm disappointed in you," her mother said. "When you
go away to college you'll remember these days, how rude
you were to me. I think you'll be sorry."

Her mother pulled in at the John/Juan taco stand. "Let's
celebrate," she said unexpectedly.

"What?"

Her mother said, "Today I am turning a corner. I am

saying good riddance to your father. I am grateful to the lettuce lady."

"What?"

They stepped into the café.

A bowl of chocolate eggs wrapped in foil sat on the counter by the cash register.

A weathered old man wearing a cowboy hat motioned to the bowl. He was the greeter. "Take, take!" he said, as they stood there for a moment. "Happy Easter!" He picked up two skinny menus and pointed to guide them to their table. Sylvia dug her hand into the bowl (no one seemed to be looking her way) and grabbed at least eight eggs. She popped them into the pocket of her jacket. If she didn't forget about them when she got home, she could make her own little basket. She could add the perfect tiny blue egg that had fallen from a nest high in the pecan tree the other day. And the necklace of colorful beads her father had left her with his pitiful good-bye note. She refused to wear it but liked how it looked. And an old Monopoly piece someone had lost in the street—the tiny silver shoe. She could make her own basket every day of her life.

Enough

When you saw a headline like that, "CIVILIANS KILLED IN INTENSIVE FIGHT FOR CITY," and did not know from those words alone how many there were, what city, what country, what they were doing at the time they were killed, how could you just wash your face and go off to school? Pretending the world was in balance? That the bell ringing in the science hallway was a real bell?

Was it their fault those civilians lived in a place where so much fighting was going on?

Civilians stacked chipped plates on a wooden shelf in the cupboard. They swept their front stone stoops with tattered brooms of ten thick straw hairs. They folded their dusty comforters. Coins jingled in a teapot with a hole. Civilians would have had more possessions if they could have, as anyone would—a better bucket, a donkey, a blue glass pitcher for juice, when there was juice, which was not often.

And now they were dead.

How could you see your friends at school and slap hands and say, "Hey man, doin' great. . . ."

Ali slipped gingerly into his desk in first period Government. Was studying government more important than ever or completely irrelevant?

What could your teacher say?

What about the window there? Shining. Why did your window deserve to shine?

The talkative girl Susan leaned across the aisle to Ali and said, "Did you take notes on that petro-political stuff yesterday and could I possibly see them after class?" She was always asking him things. Sometimes strange things, like, Is it true you don't date?

He wished he had unfolded the newspaper so he had more details—where were these civilians?—but he had only brought the paper inside, placing it tenderly on the table where his parents would find it after work.

They went out through the garage every morning when they left, traveling almost forty-five minutes to the university where they taught, so he was the one, stepping through the front door to catch the school bus down the block thirty minutes later, who brought in the paper.

They had their rituals. He placed his father's soft slippers back together as a pair and left them at his father's side of the bed. He returned his mom's bathrobe to its hook and draped the sash over it. In the evenings when he came home from debate club or chess club or the public library, where he did most of his studying, his parents would have dinner ready, rice fresh in the pot. They ate together, usually chatting somewhat formally about their days, other times in silence. If the news had been really bad near Islamabad, if more "fighters" had died in Peshawar, they were silent.

Ali had never been to Afghanistan or Iraq, but his father had been to both places, long ago, when he was a student, before this recent round of warfare had disrupted the region so thoroughly and sent battles spilling over into their own part of mountainous Pakistan. The place they all missed so much. Where his cousins were trying to study.

Ali's teacher often stared at him, as if he could tell there were thoughts swirling in turmoil inside Ali's brain. His teacher wore a concerned expression that seemed to say, "I wish you could explain this to us."

But Ali could not. War was not his interest. Studying and living seemed captivating to him, but weapons and strict ideologies which led people to fight other people left him cold.

Today their class had a substitute. Which was a good thing. Because Ali did not want to see the deep pools of his kind teacher's eyes and fall into them. He didn't know how to swim.

"The worst thing," his chemist father always said, "is infighting among citizens. They should practice local diplomacy. Get together at town meetings, work out their differences. Local pride should require presenting a better face to the world.

"To have the United States strangely present in the region is one bad thing. To have the British Parliament speaking about us as if we are merely a land of rebels and thugs is deeply painful. But to have our own people, our brother Pakistanis, bombing hotels, killing children in schools, cannot be fathomed. It is quite obvious violence is contagious as pig flu or any kind of virus."

His father's doctor had suggested an antidepressant.

His father said there was only one reasonable next phase for the wars—Get out. Get out of there, U.S. military. Take your heartless drones and go. It was not your place to be.

Not one of the grandmothers, uncles, teachers, bread sellers, shepherds had ever hurt you.

These people had no such power or interest. These people, now dead, were interested in where a greener patch of grass grew, so their goats or sheep would be happy.

Now no one was happy.

The children of the American soldiers, missing their parents, weren't happy.

The children of the British soldiers, celebrating birthdays without their dads singing to them, weren't happy.

The Pakistani kids, now dead, weren't a bit happy.

The immigrant kids worldwide, like Ali, weren't happy at all. They were confused.

Ali sometimes wished he had no imagination. It seemed a terrible, depraved thing to wish. But how was imagination helping him? He could imagine those civilians too clearly. Their voices, the salty smells of their lean, brown bodies after days in the fields, the *clip-clop* of an old man's cane against paving stones. The elegant way a checkered scarf was knotted and tied. Ali had read only yesterday that military handbooks of the United States said, "Empathy will become a weapon."

"Would you like some more?" his mother asked. The newspaper, today, lay unread on the far end of the table beyond the condiments.

"Thank you," said Ali softly. "I think I've had enough."

Weatherman

Jacob felt excited to enter the airport, even if the drive-thru and façade were so messed up by construction it looked like a disaster zone.

He mouthed the names of airlines—Continental, American—feeling proud, relieved. It had been a terrible summer so far. Get me out of here. He pulled his suitcase on its little black wheels.

When his Aunt Fanny on Martha's Vineyard had phoned his mom two weeks ago and said, "Why don't you send Jacob up here for ten days, he can help me on my computer and clean out a few closets and we'll have a great time"—he jumped on it. They even found a good cheap ticket on the internet.

Even though Aunt Fanny lived quite a distance from

everything except a giant meadow, some woods, and a pond, and the closest business to her house was a general store selling lollipops and taffy, it would be nice to feel cool sea air and be away from everyone who wasn't calling him.

Not one person had asked him to do anything all summer.

He couldn't mention this to his mother. She'd only say, But have you asked them? What would you like to do, Jacob?

He didn't know. He'd been sitting at his desk. He'd cleaned out his drawers. He'd been on Facebook. He'd sorted through his clothes and given half of them away. He should have gone to Tanzania with Matthew to build a water tank. Even studying Japanese at the junior college would have been preferable to the summer he'd had. He was sick of thinking about being a high school senior, all the work ahead of him, applying to colleges, making decisions. He should have gotten a job. Yes, he should have applied for that lovely job he saw at Target, pushing the giant snaking line of shopping carts across the 105-degree pavement. Then at least he would have had a suntan and some cash in his pocket.

Gate 35 flashed *Houston, Boston, Houston, Boston.*

He would take a bus straight from Boston's Logan Airport to Woods Hole, then a ferry to Vineyard Haven on the island. He liked how his trip sounded more and more like the journey of a leprechaun as it went along. Maybe by Woods Hole he'd be wearing a pointed red felt cap.

Aunt Fanny would meet him in her rattling green jeep.

She was the eccentric of the family, the thrice-married landscape painter with Plymouth Rock chickens wandering around her back steps and her own son teaching high school in Rabat, Morocco. Maybe Jacob could visit him next.

He'd brought along a book to read on the plane—Dave Eggers's *Zeitoun*, about the Arab-American man in New Orleans who stayed behind during the hurricane to watch his properties and help people and animals, and ended up being thrown into prison.

He sipped some Starbucks, sitting at his airplane gate, and floated on a page of text. "What are you reading?" a shockingly familiar voice spoke right into his ear. It was so familiar Jacob almost couldn't turn his head to learn where it came from. Terrifying, actually.

He lifted his gaze to his English teacher from last year— Mrs. Dunlap—smiling at him conspiratorially.

"I'm glad to see you reading, at least."

God! She was so condescending. All year she'd acted as if his opinions were little wads of trash. No respect at all. She'd given him a C on his paper about the American transcendentalists—possibly the best paper he'd ever write in his life. It deserved A+ at least. If not ++. What was she doing here?

She sniffed. "I'm very happy to be headed to Cambridge to visit my grandchildren for a week. We're going to play, play, play!"

Cambridge! That meant Boston. Horrible. He stared like a zombie at the boarding pass in her hand and saw 16A. He was 16B. You've got to be kidding.

Jacob had never had an easy time with teachers who treated him poorly. He couldn't forgive them. His mom always said he could make a stronger effort, ask for conversation after class, end up being friends. But it was hard. By the time they hit William Faulkner and Ernest Hemingway, whom he hated and loved, in that order, by the time she insulted his selection of William Burroughs as a parallel text for Faulkner ("You can't just pick people who are named William and expect there to be any connection"), by the time Tim O'Brien actually came to their school to talk about *The Things They Carried* and behaved so generously toward the students, as if they had brains and hearts, which was a major contrast to her attitude, Jacob's mood had hardened toward Mrs. Dunlap forever.

This seating arrangement was a slap in the face.

"Are you off to visit the Boston-area campuses?"

Lump in his throat. "No, I've taken a brief job on Martha's Vineyard."

"Doing?"

"Cleaning closets."

"Truly?"

"For the arts community."

"Seriously, Jacob?"

"Their closets are very dirty."

He wanted a seat change. But the flight agent had announced the flight was full—no cash or vouchers offered for anyone to stay behind. He would have taken twelve cents and waited all day not to have to sit next to Mrs. Dunlap for four hours.

She sniffed again. "I think you have a lot of potential, Jacob. More than you realize."

Sure, sure. She could go to hell.

They boarded the plane without speaking further. He had only one choice. When the flight took off, he'd go to sleep and sleep the whole way.

He pressed the button for his seat to recline the first moment he could. The air felt bumpy and unsettled. He stared out the window. Froth of cumulus, swallow me. He spoke to the clouds. Layers of subtle movement. They comforted him, just being there—they were so speechless, as he often was, and especially now, trapped in a silver tube with a woman who thought she knew him.

She unfolded her *New York Times*. "Jacob, do you have any thoughts about what you might do with your life?"

His pitiful, B-, uninspired life.

His chest felt tight.

He had never even thought of this before, but it came out of his mouth.

"Yes," he said. "I'm going to be a weatherman."

Feeding Nightmares

"Were there really alligators in there?" Sissy asked Lola, staring into the pit, and Lola said, in a voice slightly deeper than usual, "Yes, for sure. They escaped. No one knows where they are right now."

She didn't mention this had been thirty years ago.

The abandoned pit was overgrown with weeds. Stone troughs under a strange canopy that looked like an ancient mushroom. Lola, who was sixteen, and Sissy, half her age, held hands.

Sissy whispered, "How long do alligators live?"

And Lola, who had no idea, said, "Longer than people, Sissy. They have really good memories, too. They can remember people screaming at them and being mean to them and throwing things into the pit. I think they got out of here looking for revenge." Sissy's cheeks flushed pink and Lola pulled her forward toward the car.

Sissy had not quite gotten over the rats, the monkeys wearing helmets, and the snake in a suitcase—her recent nightmares, in succession. She'd wake up sobbing at two a.m. and run to their parents' bedroom, babbling tearfully. Sometimes they let her climb into bed with them, as if she were a toddler. Lola kept her own bedroom door locked. Ridiculous, really. To lose all your confidence just because the lights went out.

A few years before, Lola had read Sissy *A Rat's Tale*, by Tor Seidler, a fantastic book about the huge rodent civilization living in the sewers under New York City. Sissy didn't seem scared at the time. She seemed to love it—rats talking and mingling, rats with pocketbooks and pillows, making plans, owning Central Park after sundown.

These days, Sissy had nasty dreams about sewers. In one, she dropped her own special pink purse through the hole and rats ran off with it. She slid into a sewer's swirling torrent and nearly drowned, madly treading stinky water. Last week she had screamed in the night till their mother came running and found her covered with sweat. All she could say was, "Tell them *no!*"

Unfortunately, Sissy had recently seen real disgusting rats clinging onto a bird feeder, nibbling seed, through the window at her piano teacher's house. The rats scrambled up a tree when her teacher rapped on the glass.

Sissy had never even considered rats climbing trees. Now she worried about them jumping onto her head when she walked on sidewalks. "I saw huge cockroaches running across Jenny's kitchen floor, too. They have a very nice clean house and Jenny didn't get that excited, but I wanted to go home right away."

Around any corner, something creepy might be loitering.

Sissy was even afraid to open the cabinet under the sink to get the dish soap. Once a mouse had run out. At their uncle's farm, they'd seen the glittering eyes of spiders in a field after dark when Uncle Jack fanned his flashlight across them. Terrible!

"I think maybe she should see Michelle," their mother said to their father after supper, as Lola loaded the dishwasher, envisioning a city made of plates and glasses and cups. Her ears perked up. "She's thinking disaster every single day now. What's gotten into her? I don't even let her watch the news anymore—one bombing scene and she can't fall asleep till two a.m."

Mangled metal. Crushed bedrooms of innocent children. Blood. African deserts, skeletal families holding out empty bowls. Everything in the world that might feed your nightmares was right there in front of you, anywhere you turned.

Michelle had been their parents' marriage counselor, from the days when their father did nothing but go to work and train for long-distance bicycle rides. He'd fallen off his bike finally and they hadn't needed counseling in a while. "What does Michelle know about rats?" he asked.

"Our health teacher said there are certain fatty foods that contribute to erratic sleep," Lola said loudly. "Guacamole, for example. And ice cream. Maybe you shouldn't let her have any avocados on her salad."

Their mom sighed. "Avocados are her favorite thing."

At this moment, while she was being discussed, Sissy was upstairs in her floral bedroom cutting pink and green construction paper into long strips for her science graph. She had a chair pulled in front of her closet door, which often opened in the night by itself. Lola dried her hands and went upstairs. "You're going to therapy," she whispered to Sissy.

"What?"

"Because of your bad dreams. Once you get into therapy they give you drugs, then you get hooked on the drugs, then it takes years to get off the drugs, and by then . . ."

"Lola, is that true? I don't want drugs!"

Outside an ominous cloud had split open. Massive

raindrops plopped against the window. Perfect backdrop, Lola thought. "Maybe you should tell Mom and Dad your bad dreams have stopped. Just like that."

Sissy looked dubious.

"They're worried about you. You're acting overly sensitive, you know. And really, you're old enough at eight to ease their worries by acting a little tougher and stronger. If you wake up at night, for god's sake cut out the screaming crap, just turn on your own light and do something creative. Write a thank you letter to grandma, don't run crying to them. Then they won't make you go. "

"You think not?"

"I'm sure not. Therapy costs money. You know they'd rather save it."

Sissy stared at her. "Thank you," she said.

At breakfast the next morning, uneasy about the dumb mascara that kept smudging onto her cheeks and her expensive brown suede boots that made her trip, though she had begged for them, Lola said to Sissy, "Let's go to the zoo after school. You want to? We haven't been to the zoo in forever. Also the Japanese tea garden just reopened; we can visit the fish. And the alligator pit. Good idea? It will help you take your mind off all this stuff you've been worrying about."

Fixer-Upper

When the hailstorm hit the city at two a.m., Danni woke to one thought: Knock our house down, please.

Kindly remove the roof, flatten the walls, don't let anyone get hurt, but level it. She could picture her family plucked from the rubble by a giant crane, each saved by a perfect piece of weathered timber which had created an arc over every ramshackle bed.

Bam-bam, lemon-sized hailstones slamming the windows, the dented tin top. . . .

Maybe an insurance company would move them to the St. Anthony Hotel, where they could have room service for a month.

Why did some people live in elegant homes or sleek loft spaces while her family lived in horrible tilted nasty shacks, one after another, all their livelong days? She was sixteen and had lived in nine fixer-uppers. Lavaca, Riddle, Staffel, San Geronimo . . . at least the streets had good names. Now they lived on Sweet Street, but it wasn't.

Her father, like an undercover agent in a black shirt and black jeans, tacked WE BUY UGLY HOUSES signs to telephone poles in the middle of the night. "It's when I do my best work," he always said. He bought houses sad people were desperate to sell, people on drugs, people whose sisters needed rehab, people who had inherited the shack from a psychotic great-aunt who never painted a room in her life. And Danni's family lived in them one after another and worked on them. Paint cans and ladders in every corner. New drawer pulls in the bathroom. Danni despised the sounds of drilling and sawing. Every house they'd lived in was For Sale the whole time they lived in it. She remembered when she still imagined her father might *really* fix something up. It was ten years ago. All he did was cosmetic.

And when had she last had a friend over? You could not have people for dinner if you lived out of boxes. At Sylvie's house on Madison Street, the English floral china on the table matched, and Sylvie's mom rolled purple cloth napkins into shiny silver napkin rings. This almost made Danni cry.

Her own mom Frieda had striped hair, wore a white sweatshirt with holes in it at home, and thought she looked cool. Frieda ran the cafeteria at the courthouse and chatted with potential jurors every day. She imagined she had her finger on the pulse of the city. Every night, the same story, "I met the most fascinating person." But they were never fascinating. The bald guy who fried pies at some chain place. The philanthropist wearing a 1968 Gucci scarf. Frieda believed the jury system was great and fair, but Danni did not. She had seen her father in action. Full of slanted Big Talk, with nothing to back any of it up. Although he did not commit actual crimes that she knew of, she could hardly imagine him in a position to decide another person's fate. He would think of the best deal. He would stretch truth, counting his pennies.

Something crashed in the kitchen. Danni got up, slipped into moccasins, and tiptoed to see. A tiny blue glass vase had fallen from the windowsill and smashed on the floor. She looked for a broom. It was always so hard to find anything useful. She wondered if it were safe to be that close to the window herself. GIRL BEHEADED BY FLYING WINDOW!

Thunder crashing crazily outside, and where was the rest of her family? How could they sleep through such a storm? She was the family brooder. They never let her forget it.

Her sisters, twins two years older than she, were counting down till graduation. The week after, on the fifth of June, they'd be moving together to Spain. Both swimming champions, already they had jobs at some sleek swim resort. What would she do without them?

They told her moving so often wasn't that bad. "We get new neighbors—enjoy it!" They shared a bedroom while she was stuck alone. They made their rooms look cute and comfy even if their dad had found their enormous shared dresser in a trash heap on Guadalupe Street. Danni kept a trunk at the foot of her bed, also found at a dump, which she had painted with blue stars.

"And what about college?" she asked them, jealously. "When will you go? What if you like your jobs too much?"

"Later!" they said. "We'll have adventures, make money, perfect our Spanish, find rich Spanish boyfriends, then go to college when we're twenty! Everyone goes to college too soon."

Danni stared out at the crooked back deck to watch hailstones banging against the cat's bowl, the turtle's tub. Where were the cat and turtle? She could hardly go outside to look for them—she'd get a concussion. What would it be like to be a turtle inside a shell hit by hailstones?

To know exactly what you wanted to do after graduation?

To have a father with a normal job?

A biology teacher? Insurance executive? Vet?

Oh, how she wished her father were a vet! Fixer-upper

Animal Bodies instead of Fixer-upper Houses. Right now he owned two houses on Vance Street, three on Echo, two on Theo. She would sometimes drive with him to check on their security. Ha! He asked her to plant yellow marigolds in an empty pot on the porch of a hut, thinking it might increase his chance of reselling it for three thousand dollars more than he had paid. She told him what she'd read—that frying onions or baking an apple pie in the kitchen, when someone was coming to look at your house, was the biggest boon toward a sale. It made people feel cozy and optimistic to smell those things. Like something good was happening. He looked thoughtful. She wanted to cry. How could you bake an apple pie without a stove?

Break

Shoes still wrapped in soft beige tissue in a box, black suede with a slick leather sole, ballet pump style. Her mother had mentioned the price being too high, but bought them anyway. Why hadn't Lou worn them yet? Everyone else wore them. What was she saving them for?

Confidence, a quarter she used to carry in her deepest pocket. One day it just wasn't there.

Hair, pulled back or braided. Maybe it was time for a big trim. At certain points things weighed you down.

She was not my teacher.

All her classmates were attending the memorial service for Ms. Vogt, but Lou had forgotten about it and arrived at school after the buses left. It was pretty amazing that an entire high school would shut down so everyone could go to

the service in a very large church. Couldn't they have con-
ducted the funeral at the school?

Her dad had dropped her off. Lou didn't remember
what was happening, why the parking lot appeared so
vacant, till she found no one in the front hallway and walked
down to the English wing to find it deserted as fairgrounds
after the fair had left. So Lou sat on a bench outside near the
locked library and closed her eyes. The library door had a
sign: LIBRARY CLOSED TILL TUESDAY AFTERNOON.

It was too far to walk to the church.

Lonely. Horrible. Ms. Vogt had fallen out the window
of her second-floor classroom. Ms. Vogt had died at school.

This was why everyone was taking her death so hard.

What the heck was she doing?

No one was supposed to open the windows at school
because of the air-conditioning, but there were stories about
Ms. Vogt—she had asthma, hated refrigerated air, got too
cold. Someone said she often stood in the old-fashioned tall
windowsill of the class to demonstrate a point in literature.
Could it be? What teacher would do that? Her students
adored her—she loved dialogue and passionate literary
interpretation more than the insulting standardized require-
ments of tests now dominating the world of public schools.
Ms. Vogt wrote letters to the editor about how teachers were

being disrespected. Why can't teachers be trusted to know what's most important to teach our students? Where are creative strategies, if everything is prescribed? Other teachers admired her. She didn't seem afraid of being fired.

Just as she resisted clichés in education, it was widely known that Ms. Vogt hated clichés in speech and writing, which was why Lou felt relieved she had not been her teacher.

Lou had become a walking, talking, hair-brushing cliché. Maybe it happened at fourteen, maybe fifteen. She wished she could pinpoint the moment and revise it, delete backward to a better self.

How could she ever find again what she had lost?

That freshness of early childhood, when she never fell into ruts of speech, never said "whatever" or "see if I care," which she could blame on her cousin Andi, who was always saying it, as well as something stupid about smelling the roses, and what about that horrible memory of the day she realized she was simply a stooge?

It had been Activity Day on the playing field, everyone dressed for sports, high-jumping, long-jumping, running track—Lou's favorite nightmare.

Her event, junior volleyball, was the fallback event for girls in her class who were not the least bit athletic. Lou was embarrassed at the way she often dodged the ball instead of punching it. The ball scared her. She didn't want to break her wrist. And today they had to play with people watching.

Dad is a runner. Mom used to be a runner. What is my problem?

Lou was terrible at everything. Including, apparently, expression. When Ms. Vogt walked past her on Activity Day, buff in navy running shorts and a red tank, she smiled and said, "Hey there, when does your turn come?"

Lou said, "Oh, I'm just in volleyball; we're last, last but not least, I guess."

Ms. Vogt had said, "Oh my! Give up the cliché, dear—there's a good habit to break right now. Good luck!"

She had reached out to touch her arm, smiled benevolently, and walked on, leaving Lou confused.

What had Lou said, exactly? She had to replay her own words in her mind, and was still feeling shaken when her event was announced.

On the volleyball court, she tripped, stumbled, and knocked one of her own teammates very hard with her elbow. At least she didn't break anything. Her team lost and no one even slapped hands or said, "Good game" when it was over, because it was not a good game at all. Nawal Khan, her friend from Abu Dhabi who had played equally badly on their team, said, "That may have been the worst game in the history of sports." She laughed, but Lou couldn't laugh.

Later, any time Lou passed Ms. Vogt, she turned her head away.

It was terrible when a single conversation with someone determined your whole future relationship.

She thought about visiting Ms. Vogt at lunchtime someday to ask, "How does one avoid it exactly? The world of clichés? Because they are everywhere around us and they are very aggressive."

But she was afraid Ms. Vogt would make fun of her.

So, how had such a confident teacher fallen out the window of her own classroom?

This was not a clichéd death. It was an original one.

Are We Friends?

Callie stepped into a yellow taxi at the Chicago airport and gave the address of the hotel where she and her teacher would be convening for the Poetry Out Loud national finals. Her teacher had been concerned when they couldn't travel together, but Callie wasn't worried at all. She knew how to get places. She was using her dad's frequent flyer miles and took a different airline. All the way she'd been saying her three memorized poems inside her head.

"Where are you coming from?" the driver greeted her. There was snow beside the road.

"Corpus Christi."

Turned out he had once lived in the same Texas coastal town where Callie lived now.

She said, "That's crazy! So, do you get back down to Texas?"

"I do"—he paused—"but the whole coast is ruined."

They were stopped at a light. Callie thought he might be referring to smokestacks spewing residue, stretching suburbs, the shrinking shrimp population. . . .

He said, "They've built three mosques."

"What?"

"And they work in all the gas stations and quick shops, too."

She'd been in his car less than five minutes. His meaning hit her. That unattended "they." He was driving a little too fast, too.

"You mean, Arabs? Muslims?" She could see his pale eyes in the rearview mirror staring at her.

He nodded.

She gulped and paused. "Well, my dad is an Arab . . . from a Muslim family . . . and he's adorable. Not very religious in any way, but super sweet. You might like him."

The driver swerved. Pulled to the side of the road, took his foot off the pedal. Callie thought he might be throwing her out. But he turned his head around.

"I'm so sorry! Please forgive me. Are you mad at me?"

It was strange. A man passed on the sidewalk with a poodle in a pink sweater on a leash. Callie said, "I'm not mad. . . . I guess I'm just sad, though."

She didn't know what to say. The driver accelerated slowly again, pulling back into traffic. She said, "Haven't you ever known any nice Arabs?"

He said, "You are really mad, aren't you? I'm sorry. I talk too much."

Callie said, "Haven't you?" She was thinking about prejudice, how it might begin so simply—*they come from elsewhere, they don't look the way I do*. Why did people want to match? And here they were in the great multicultural city of the first African-American but also half-white U.S. president in history.

Callie slumped in the seat.

The driver said, "My girls are in Eye-rack."

"What?"

"They're nurses. They don't see much action. Frankly, they're in it for the money. And they met some nice Arabs, they said."

Callie said, "Wow. Were they wounded?"

"My daughters?"

"No, the Arabs. You said your daughters are nurses?"

"Yes. Wounded. Your dad is really an Arab?"

She sighed. "Yes. From Syria and Lebanon both. He hates war. He grew up in too many wars. He'd feed you even if you didn't like him."

The driver said, "He'd feed me?"

"He likes to feed people."

The driver was silent again. They passed a Jamaican coffee shop, a Korean Bar-B-Q, a Vietnamese diner. They passed grandmas of indeterminate origin wrapped in fluffy black coats. They passed shoe shops, a burned-out factory, and an apartment building with faded graffiti streaking the sides.

Then he said, "Oprah Winfrey is not as good-looking as she appears on TV."

Callie started laughing. "Oprah is *gorgeous*! My mom gets *O* magazine—she looks fantastic on every cover. Do you know her?"

"I've driven her. They really make her up. Airbrush. And she's too rich! No one should be that rich."

"Yeah, well, she gives a lot of it away. Isn't that good?"

"And Julia Roberts is not really blond. She has dark roots."

Callie laughed out loud. What a complainer.

Then she said, "I'll bet I know one person we could agree on."

"Who's that?"

"Elizabeth Smart—she's brave. She was so great to speak up for herself and all victims in court. And the guy who kidnapped her is horrible and the same goes for that disgusting man in California who kidnapped the other girl and kept her in his yard." Then Callie realized she should probably stop talking about kidnapping to a prejudiced individual with his hands on the wheel.

"I'm with you," he said. "Okay, we now agree."

Again they drove in silence. Past more old buildings, ponds, ducks, trees wearing golden autumn sweaters. Every city, a mosaic of blocks and hopes and ash cans and bright signs. Callie thought of the Langston Hughes poem she'd wished she could include in the contest, but it wasn't long enough. It began, "I can see your house, babe, but I can't see you." Inside her head she said, Yo Langston, man, you really told the truth.

"Are we friends now?" the driver asked. He was driving better.

"We were never not friends," Callie said. "I'm just keeping my fingers crossed you meet some really great Arabs soon."

He said, "See, you're still mad."

When they arrived at her hotel, he jumped out to retrieve her suitcase from the back. She paid him and tried to give him a tip, but he pushed it away.

"No tip, since I insulted you," he said. "I couldn't."

"Yes, you could," Callie said. "But I only want you to do one thing with it. Buy some really good coffee from a nice Arab. And I hope your daughters get home safely and soon."

He took the money. Stood there awkwardly, as if he wanted to say something else. Which he did. "My wife . . . is from Mexico."

Great Wall

"Today my mom told me she's fine now and can stop taking her bipolar drug. And I went bipolar. No, Mom, you can't! You need to take it forever."

She said, "Do you really think my well-being depends on a little pill?"

"Yes, I do," I said. "I really really do. And, having known you all my life, so does mine." Sarah covered her face with her hands.

A truck backed up outside, making its back-up beep. How appropriate.

Margaret, the therapist, smiled, said nothing.

Sarah just kept talking. "She told me I was being dramatic. She said I should give her another chance to do it herself. She makes it seem as if I'm responsible for her being on drugs. Helpful drugs. As if she's only doing it for me, not for herself. I really hate that. Because I have only one more year at home, and Dad's already left, so who's she going to take her drugs for after I leave? Will I just be worrying about her forever?"

"Yes," said Margaret. "You will always be worrying. It's human nature and especially your nature. But do you really think she plans to quit her medication? We need to get her to her own doctor immediately if that's the case."

"I don't know," said Sarah. "She might already have stopped taking it. She might be lying."

"I thought she never lies."

"She never used to. But she started, once she was feeling better."

"What else did she lie about?"

"Her boyfriends. I thought they were just piano students. But now I think they're all her boyfriends."

"How old are they again?"

"Oh, in their late teens and twenties. About twenty years younger than my mom. I thought they were all gay. But I came home the other evening unexpectedly and there were yellow roses on the kitchen table and one of them was in the bathroom and he doesn't even have his lesson that day."

"Did you ask her?"

"Of course I asked her. She said they were celebrating

his new job at some restaurant or something. They were eating shrimp."

"Sarah, what do you want from your mother?"

"Me? I want her to be stable!"

"But what do you want her to give *you*? Why are you so angry at her?"

"Angry? I'm not angry!"

"Are you sure? Angry because your dad left? What do you blame that on?"

"Her, definitely her."

"Does he speak to you about it?"

"Whenever I can catch him in the U.S. of A."

Sarah cringed. That was definitely another thing she had gotten from her mother.

Stupid phrases.

"She blames everything on him. I've always been their captive audience. It's so exhausting."

"And would you like her to release you from that position at this point?"

"Of course I would."

"Do you realize you may have to release yourself?"

"You mean just walk out the door when I go to college in Vermont or Washington state, whichever farther corner of the country will have me?"

"No. I mean, emotionally. Once and for all, inside

yourself. Saying, I am not your audience. I am not your sounding board. I am Sarah and you are Angie and Dad is Max and we are each responsible for the well-being of our own minds and spirits."

"Sounds great. Has never been true even for a minute."

"So let's find a way to work with that."

Sarah glanced at her watch. Sure, in the last four seconds, let's find a way. Let's come back another day. Let's be bound together now, you and I, as if I were a little donkey and you are the cart I am pulling as you tug on the reins and direct me, right or left, stop or go.

Max was in China hiking on the Great Wall. He'd finished a consulting job in Beijing and had a few days off. He wished Sarah were with him. No one else was at the Great Wall because Chinese people, apparently, did not like to freeze their butts off in winter by taking stupid outdoor hikes. Even the sky ride operator, who ferried people up to the top of the wall from the parking lot, had gone home while Max was walking, so he had to climb all the way down by himself, finding the big stone steps among frozen bushes, keeping himself oriented. The sun was sinking, cold deepening, eerie silence cropping up. You could imagine armies plotting against you in a silence like that. No, you could imagine all the mistakes you'd ever made, laughing at you. What if he got lost and couldn't make it back to his taxi waiting in the lot? What would happen then?

I thought about you, Sarah, he wrote later in his e-mail. *Your dad afraid, doing something dumb, going to the Wall too late in the day. Who imagines being alone up there? Quite surreal.*

Her father wrote better than he talked, sometimes. So sometimes it wasn't bad that he was far away.

But I made it! Here I am, your dad on earth, for another day!

To her mom he wrote perfunctory notes—Work went well, must stay two extra days for flight changes.

Maybe that was part of the problem.

If you didn't tell your story in the most interesting way you might, how was someone else expected to care?

So Sarah used to tell her mom how cool Max was and that didn't work, either.

"You like your father better than you like me."

"Someday, I will not be a bridge," Sarah thought, walking to her car from Margaret's office. "Someday I too will be the Great Wall. I will stand quietly in the sunset, turning different colors. I will separate the tangled past from the future. I will be nice to children."

Allied with Green

For her paper on What I Believe In, Lucy writes first "the color green."

That's how everything starts. A tiny shoot of phrase prickling the mind . . .

Then she runs around for a few days doing other things but noticing the green poking up between buildings, on sides of roads, in front of even the poorest homes, how pots of green lined on rickety front porches, hanging baskets of green on light posts downtown, the new meticulous xeriscape beds of puffy green grasses and plants alongside the river, are what seem to keep everything else going. If people could not see green from the windows of the hospital, the hospital might fall down. She believes this.

Once she starts making a list, it will not stop.

Green has had a terrible summer. Threatened by the longest drought and highest heat in recorded history, green has had many second thoughts.

Lucy's family could only water with a sprinkler on Wednesday evenings between eight and ten. When she and her mom wash lettuce, blueberries, peaches, they carry the plastic tubs of fruit water outside to pour onto a plant. It's ritual now. It's holy water. The city had a water waster hotline. It made the national news. You could turn people in for excessive watering.

Last semester, when asked to write a paper on addictions, Lucy wrote about trimming and got a C. Her teacher scrawled across the top of the paper, "What is this?" But Lucy often feels happiest with pruning shears in her hand, heading toward an overgrown jasmine vine.

It's a clear task, trimming. The longer you've done it, the more you know how it encourages green, in the long run. Also, you can have fine ideas while trimming. Queen's crown, germander, plumbago. *Snip, snip, snip.*

She knew it had been mentioned before, but thought she ought to include how cities assault their green for two reasons: money and greed. Later, feeling remorseful, or sickened by the new view, they name everything for green—Oak Meadows, Lone Pine. You could find it almost anywhere now.

Lucy's father demonstrated against developments when

he was in college. She had a faded black and white picture of him holding a NO! sign, his hair bushy and wild. Highways slashing through green space—he now drives one of those highways almost every day, feeling guilty. He plants free trees in scrappy medians, as an apology. Sometimes people steal them. When he planted four little palms in pots as a gift to Freddy's Mexican Restaurant, they got plucked from the soil overnight. Obviously some people were desperate for green. And surely, with all the population issues now, some developments were necessary, but look at what happened before you knew it—hills sheared, meadows plucked, fields erased, the world turns into an endless series of strip centers—yo, Joni Mitchell! Joni sang about parking lots when the world had probably half the number it has now. Her dad told her that. She likes Joni Mitchell.

The boulevard wakes up when a strip of green is planted down its center.

The sad room smiles again when a pot of green is placed on a white tablecloth.

No one goes to Seattle to see the concrete.

An exhausted kid says, I'm going outside—sick of her mother's voice, she knows she will feel better with bamboo.

In Dallas people run around the lake or refresh themselves at the arboretum.

San Antonians send their kids to summer digging classes

at the botanical gardens. The kids come home with broccoli. After a while.

Patience is deeply involved with green.

It's required.

So, why don't people respect green as much as they should?

This was the serious question growing small fronds and tendrils at the heart of Lucy's paper. She knew her teacher might turn a snide nose up at it. Oh, blah blah, isn't this rather a repeat of what you wrote last semester?

People took green for granted. They assumed it would always be skirting their ugly office buildings and residences and so they didn't give it the attention it deserved. Somewhat like air. Air and green, close cousins.

Lucy truly loved the words *pocket park*.

She loved community gardeners with purple bandannas tied around their heads. She loved their wild projects—rosemary grown so big you could hide in it.

She loved roofs paved with grass.

She loved the man in New York City—Robert Isabell—who planted pink impatiens on the metal overhang of his building. He had started out as a florist, at seventeen, in Minnesota—green state in the summer, not so green in December. Then he moved to New York City and became a major party planner, incorporating flowers, lighting, tents, fabrics, to create magical worlds of festivity. He didn't attend his own parties. He disappeared once he got everything set up. Sometimes he hid behind a giant potted plant to see what people liked. Lucy found his obituary in the newspaper, clipped it out, and placed it on her desk. She wished she could have worked for him just to learn how he put flowers together on tables, how he clipped giant green stalks and placed them effectively around a tent to make Morocco, Italy, the French Riviera. Transporting. Green could take you away.

Save you. But you had to care for it, stroke it, devote yourself to it, pray to it, organize crews for it, bow down to it. You had to say the simple holy prayer, rearranging the words any way you liked best—"Dig, Grow, Deep, Roots, Light, Air, Water, Tend."

Tend was a more important verb than most people realized.

You had to carry a bucket.

His Own Voice

It was exactly one year to the day since her father died. Every twenty-second of every month had a sting to it, but this was the one-year sting and it was bigger. She'd ridden her bike to San Fernando Cathedral that morning to light a candle, though her father was not Catholic, and she wasn't, either. Had he ever even entered the place? A candle cost one dollar now. She stuffed her quarters into the metal tube. Old Mexican women sat scattered in pews, praying with their heads bent. She would ride all over town today. Back streets, see what houses were for sale. Pick up some avocado-cucumber sushi with brown rice and have a quiet meal in his memory in the park. Watch the fat orange fish swirl around in murky water for a while. Some had large polka dots on them. Her mom was out of town. She might do a few errands or watch the little kids swing at the Mulberry playground.

A man stepped up to her at Broadway Daily Bread. "Your father is still alive in my phone."

Jolt.

Tall, lean man, combed-back dark hair. She'd never seen him before. He flipped his phone open. Reeled through the names to her father's and held the small screen in front of her face. Her dad's old familiar phone number still standing calmly like a small city of sevens and threes.

The man said, "You don't know me, but I recognize you. I saw you two together at the accordion festival . . . your dad and I were such good friends. We went to lunch all the time, talked regularly. I miss him so much. I still can't believe it."

Oh.   Oh.

Rainey whispered, "And your name is?"

He said, "Selim. I kept his messages as long as I could, then they disappeared. I wish they were still in here."

She thought, My father had his own life.

She wanted to hold the man's phone up and proclaim to everyone in the bakery, "My father is alive!"

Selim hugged her and said, "Take care of yourself." She left the bakery smiling.

My dad is in the sack of wheat, this birdseed bread that he loved, the street he knew, the towering pecan trees, the stop sign. . . .

Pedaling toward the park, she couldn't believe she'd forgotten to tell the man what day it was. One year exactly. Did it matter? Did he need to know?

She wondered, Would some people call him an angel? She didn't. She called him a really nice man with perfect timing. That was enough.

At home later, feeling well exercised, soaked in sun and happier than she thought she could feel on such a gloomy anniversary (Leo had offered to meet her somewhere, but she wanted to be alone all day), Rainey was surprised to find a message on her home machine from someone she hadn't talked to in two years. Annie, from Comfort Arts Camp. Annie said, "Hey! Call me back. Soon! You probably have a cell, but I don't know the number. I need to tell you something you might want to hear."

Annie's first question was, "How is your dad?"

Rainey gulped. "Did you *know* my dad?"

"Don't you remember, when he picked you up at camp, he was so nice to me and gave me that George Strait CD he had, because it was one I wanted?"

Rainey didn't remember. Maybe she'd run back inside the cabin for something she'd forgotten. Her dad was always being nice to everybody. Then she gulped. "He is dead, I'm sorry to tell you. Really really sorry."

There was a long silence. Birds sang in that silence. They sang and they stopped singing.

Annie whispered into the phone, "So now I know."

"What?"

"Why I had this dream."

"What dream?"

"Your father told me to tell you something."

"But you only saw him once."

"I realize that."

Rainey's first impulse was almost rude. She wanted to say, "Why would my father send a message through *you*? He met you once. Why wouldn't he speak directly to *me*?"

But she said, "Tell me."

"He said to tell you he's fine. He's really fine. Everything is fine."

"Could you see him when he said this?"

"Of course I could. That's how I recognized him. But I didn't know—what happened, you know. I thought, maybe you two just had a fight or something."

"We never fought," Rainey whispered. Long, long pause. Then, "You saw him."

Rainey had not seen her father even once in a dream,

which surprised her. She'd always thought you'd dream incessantly about the people you loved most.

"But there's something else, too," Annie said. "It's as if he kept talking in my head after I got up today. He kept saying, Call her right now."

"Wow. Well, this is the day."

"What?"

"The day he died, a year ago."

"Seriously?"

Another long silence.

Rainey whispered, "Yeah."

Annie said, "Well, I didn't tell you after camp, because it might have sounded jealous or something, but your dad seemed like the dad I always wished I had. I thought about him after we met that day. I thought, that's the dad."

"Well, now nobody has him."

"That's not true. You still have him. Inside your blood and bones and DNA. Your memory and all that. I'm sorry, Rainey. I'm kind of in shock. But you really *still have him*."

"I know. I guess I know. But he can't pick up the phone."

Rainey thought of Selim's phone. Maybe they should go to lunch. She could ask him questions. It would be like visiting with a proxy. Could she find him again? Was it possible her father was really communicating with her through such unexpected delegates?

Horizon

Jake said, "Sometimes divorce is *not* a negative. Sometimes it is like, you know, things are going to get better now."

Margot was crying in the front seat of his car. They were trying to go into a movie, *Amelia*, but she had blurted the bad news right after he picked her up at her very quiet house. Jake had noticed, walking up the sidewalk to ring her bell, that her house looked darker than usual—no lights in the upstairs bedrooms, not even the porch light turned on. She'd started sobbing as they ascended the ramp to the highway, and cried all the way to the theater. Now it looked as if they might miss the previews for sure. He really loved previews, even when they told too much and overdosed on volume. Sometimes he watched previews he loved on his computer over and over again, just to note the editing elements.

Maybe it wasn't the best night to see a movie in which one of the main characters disappeared.

Mostly Margot seemed upset because she had had no idea her parents were this close to splitting up. She always felt in touch with what was going on around her—extreme attentiveness, very important trait. Jake called her the Detail Queen and she liked it. But she had really been in the dark on this one.

Sure, her parents argued, but mostly she would have called it pernicious squabbling, not big fights in which people threw things or slammed doors. Sure, they spent regular periods away from each other (her father was a pilot—which now seemed another reason, thought Jake, they shouldn't see this movie) but that was his *job*, and no, she had never dreamed her mom could be attracted to a flight attendant she'd met at a company party. Weren't those guys usually gay? No, she shouldn't say that. She was trying to catch herself any time she stereotyped anything, even people who shopped at Target as if it were a cultural endeavor, or women with too many children under the age of five.

"I wish they'd let me in on it sooner," she sobbed.

Jake said, "Why?"

"Because it's like a slap in the face, thinking you have a regular family, then finding out you don't."

"But aren't half the families in America divorced by now?"

His certainly was. His parents had divorced when he was in middle school, and it wasn't so horrible. In fact, it was easier dealing with only one of them at a time.

Margot gasped. "I'm moving to Dubai."

"What?"

"My dad flies there and he says the buildings are incredible and cute boys from Holland play Frisbee on the beach."

Now Jake felt slapped. She would talk about "cute boys" to him? Who was this person in his vehicle? He gulped and tried to gather his wits.

"Margot, you just need to let the news settle in, and maybe it won't even happen. Sometimes parents say things that never happen after all."

"Do yours?"

He thought about it. "Not really."

People were walking past his car into the theater. Happy dates holding hands. Long-married people, the women pulling shawls tightly around their shoulders. It was always so cold in theaters.

"Are you ready to go in?" Jake asked.

Margo sniffed. "I may never be ready to do anything again."

"Your parents love you."

"Ha! That's what they said. Obviously they haven't had a thought about me in months."

"Would you rather see a different movie? I'm not attached to *Amelia* at all."

"I love Hilary Swank and Richard Gere."

"Yeah, but the reviews were pretty weak. It said, like, a script written by the same guys who write CliffsNotes."

"Don't we love CliffsNotes? They're like previews. Or after views or whatever."

He kissed her on the side of her head, above the ear. Her hair smelled peachy.

"We could see the Michael Jackson movie."

"That's really happy."

"I heard it's great." Jake looked at his watch, then the leaves scattering in the parking lot. "Or, we could just go back downtown and take a walk by the river and get hot chocolate or something. If you are not in the mood for a movie."

"No, I need a movie. I need to forget my life and fly away. Well, maybe not fly. I need someone else's troubles."

They stood in line behind three boys who were seeing the Michael Jackson movie. One wore a T-shirt that said "Michael Forever" in glittering script, with a silhouette of Michael's face. Margot thought it was really terrible what had happened to him—it seemed so preventable some-how—as in, why didn't he just hire a spectacular massage therapist with lavender oil to stand by at his bedside night and day when he couldn't sleep and sing him lullabies? She wished she had been a bigger fan of his songs while he was alive. Mostly she liked his dance steps—how he slid and scooted and skated across a stage. It was inspiring just to think of a human body with so much high-velocity potential.

Jake said, "I think all the movies may be equally depressing right now."

Amelia aka Hilary was wearing a leather flight jacket in the poster. She looked tough and hopeful. She had a weird haircut. She could go anywhere, cross any horizon, do anything. No one could stop her.

Thoreau Is My Partner

Andy's father Roberto said, "Are you sure you don't need anything? Room service? I could order eggs for you before I go?"

"No thanks." Andy rolled over in the other bed. "I'm not hungry yet. I'll find something when I get hungry." He could feel his father standing in front of the mirror without even opening his eyes. "When will you be back again?"

"Well, we have that luncheon, so I have to stay at the conference center—I may not see you before four or five, that okay?"

"That's great. I mean, fine. Perfect."

It was so rare to have a completely free day in a city where you did not live.

Andy wanted to wander. Cross the streets in Austin,

Texas. Gaze at trees poking out of improbably small strips
of soil between sidewalk and street. Sit by the state capitol
on a bench as office workers stepped out for lunch. Imagine
other lives. Check out music club posters, see who was playing. When you lived in Brownsville, way south in the giant
state of Texas, Austin seemed like the distant northern land
of Oz. Huge university, now hard to get into. Orange sweat-
shirts. Metropolis.

His father closed the door softly, saying, "Have fun!"

Andy knew he was lucky.

None of his friends' fathers said, "Have fun." They said,
"Be careful, don't get in trouble."

Andy jumped from his puffy white hotel bed. Why
didn't he have a bed like this at home? He could have slept
till ten. At 7:50, he felt ready for a shower, then to hit the
streets, find a breakfast taco, see girls. Austin girls. See guys
more cosmopolitan than he was. See anyone. Homeless
people wrapped in old blankets sleeping in the doorway
of St. David's Church. They'd walked past them last night
on the way back from dinner to the glossy AT&T Center
Hotel where the coffee tables in the giant lobby were made
of vertical pecan branches chopped to the same height and
topped with glass. The branches had been cut from trees at
the site where the hotel now stood. That didn't seem like
something to feature, but the tables were eye-catching.

Exotic plum-colored lilies or orchids in gigantic glass vases, submerged entirely in water. They were so beautiful they looked fake. Andy bumped one of the vases gently with his thumb to see if the water sloshed and it did.

It was the fanciest hotel Andy had ever stayed in. His dad had taken him to meetings in other Texas cities over the years, when Andy didn't have school. Too bad for his mom, unable to get off work till Thanksgiving day; she would have loved those lilies.

Because this was the AT&T Center, their room had more capabilities than many rooms. What looked like a radio promised to do all sorts of other things, if you punched buttons. Send food. Send help. Even the telephone welcomed them by name on a small phone-screen: "Mr. Roberto Martinez, welcome to the AT&T Center, please let us know what we can do to make your visit more enjoyable."

Find me a girlfriend? thought Andy. Get me into UT when I graduate?

He tied his tennis shoes. A cream-colored cardboard coaster next to the telephone caught his eyes. "Live each season as it passes; breathe the air, drink the drink, taste the fruit, and resign yourself to the influences of each. *Henry David Thoreau, 1817–1862*"

They'd just been reading from Thoreau's "Civil Disobedience" in school, well-chosen because many people down at the Texas border were attempting various sorts of disobedience regarding the border fence—marching, speaking out, planting crops that continued on both sides of the fence, purchasing billboards against it, building ladders taller than it.

It seemed a bit odd to have Thoreau's words in such a high-tech room. Mix it up, mix it up.

An orange poster on the wall advertised the Austin Varsity Circus, which seemed to have taken place seventy years ago. Andy wished he could have seen it.

He liked tents. Really big tents with dozens of stakes and poles and ropes, the kind circuses used to be in, like Fellini's *La Strada* tent. Tents fascinated him. What if countries made border tents instead of border fences? Cultural-exchange tents, foods and curios from each country traded, bartered, exchanged . . . there were so many more imaginative things people might do in the world than take drugs and shoot one another. He popped a Thoreau coaster into his pocket.

Out on the extremely chilly street, he wished for a muffler and a cap. Maybe that's what he'd buy—a stocking cap, thug style. The headline on a rack of *Austin American Statesman* newspapers said, "110 DIE IN BAGHDAD BOMBING." And Andy had to stop walking for a moment and place his hands over his ears.

Could anyone else hear it?

He felt as if he heard screams from the other side of the world. It was his one secret power.

He'd always felt it. When he was small, his family visited some humble mountain villages in Mexico with his mother's church group at Christmas. They dispensed fresh American socks and denim jackets, and he heard a very old woman moaning in her house. People said she was dying. For the whole next year, whenever he tried to sleep back at home, he felt he could still hear her moan. When did she die? One day he stopped hearing it.

Baghdad. Austin. He passed bars and museums. In some places the whole sidewalk smelled like beer.

Live each season as it passes... Well, what else could anyone do? Live the future? Live history? He crossed the street.

Don't Want To Talk About It

Maria found it impossible to believe she would never see him again.

Never, never, never. The terrible fact would clutch at her chest when she walked home from work in the evenings. A brick wall slapped in front of her along the path. She would have to stop walking. Close her eyes, conjure his voice in her ear. "Hey you." His musical drawl. Never. Never. He was not coming back, he was gone, she could not reach him even if she stretched her arms out for the rest of her days.

In the park across the street, a middle-aged man in a long beige raincoat paused for his little dog. Although the man looked angular and intelligent, like a person who might be walking a golden retriever or German shepherd, he had a stupid-looking fluff ball. Why did Maria imagine this mysterious man, whom she had been seeing from a distance for years, would know what she was talking about? She had never noticed him with another human being, only that dog.

Obviously, someone was lost for him, too. If you lived to be that old and only walked with a fluff ball, never another person—bad news.

"What may I get for you?" All day Maria repeated the same question over and over to everyone who approached the counter at SIP.

"Latte double shot. Decaf cappuccino. Blueberry muffin. Blah blah blah."

"I am so sick of coffee," she said to Lucky, at the silver sink, where they washed the pitchers. He worked the afternoon shift with her. He drank only tea. She preferred water with no ice. Tepid water. What was wrong with her?

"Personally I am sick of people treating us as if we are just fixtures," Lucky said.

"What do you mean?"

"As if we have time to listen to their troubles while they are making up their minds. Today a woman yakked endlessly about losing her car keys. I had to nod and be pleasant. She had a ring of keys in her hand so obviously she had found them again and anyway, what did I care? I am a coffee man, not a counselor for bimbos."

"Don't say *bimbos*."

"I'll say anything I like, sweetheart."

"Don't say *sweetheart*."

James had also called her sweetheart. She was his little sister, his shadow, his personal FBI agent, always tracking him, worrying about him, leaving him messages on his voice mail. When she begged him not to hang out with Rusty and Chad, because they seemed tough in a way James was not, he said, "Sweetheart, I don't want to talk about it. Have I selected your friends this month?"

She had had a very bad feeling. One of those intuition things she trusted and James placed no stock in.

Maria was taking a year off between high school and full-time college. For now, she took two community college courses in the evenings—Cultural Anthropology and Physical Geography, and wondered why everyone in the city didn't attend community college—it was cheap and inspiring; people didn't realize what they were missing. Her high school counselor had suggested it—she should write that woman a thank you letter.

"Don't you think it's amazing what aboriginal people of Australia have suffered and we almost never hear about it up here?" she asked Lucky. He stared at her. They didn't hear about a lot of things. When she wasn't making coffee, she was in class or studying. Her parents were mad at her. After James died, she had moved out of their sad home piled with junk mail and broken parts and clipped recipes her mother would never really make, to a minimalist apartment down the street, a single room costing $450 a month. "What a waste of money! You are four blocks from your own bedroom! Why don't you save your money for next year?"

It was hard to explain.

She could not be in the same rooms with their sadness. She could not sleep there. The weight was too heavy.

Separate sadness was worth whatever it cost. But of course they worried about her double time now, since she had become their only child. "Do you have a deadbolt on your door?"

"Please give me a sign," she whispered to James, up into the air. "A sign you are still in the atmosphere, like rain particles or toxic waste. Please check in with me. I need to know that. I am so lost."

He had left her all his money. He actually had a will in an envelope in his desk drawer, which disturbed their parents. He left her nine thousand dollars saved since the days he was a newspaper delivery boy rolling papers, poking them into plastic wrappers.

Why would anyone with enough stamina to be a newspaper delivery boy get talked into driving a getaway car for two horrible thieves? It made no sense at all. Did James even know what he was doing?

He was the only one who got shot.

When Maria walked into her tiny bare apartment, she noticed her favorite picture of James, as a twelve-year-old perfect person with all his life still ahead of him, in the middle of the floor. Usually she kept this picture on a small shelf above the bathroom sink, so she could look at it first thing in the morning and before bed.

There was absolutely no way the picture could have traveled from the bathroom to the center of her single room by itself. Even if a gale wind had been blowing through an open window (all the windows were closed). No way.

She picked it up, placed her lips right on it, held it out and said, "Thank you, James. You heard me. You were always a good brother. But was I right about those guys? I miss you horribly. What else can you do?"

Interest

"Guess what we saw," said Sam when he and their dad got back from Washington, D.C. "Mennonites on the Metro. Drinking Sprite. Did you know Mennonites drink Sprite?"

Adrienne stared at him. "I didn't even know they ride the Metro."

"Dad did great. His speech was terrific. At the National Building Museum, when he was accepting his award, I noticed he was standing on a dollar bill. After the ceremony, I went behind the podium and picked it up and kept it." He flashed the crumpled, dirty bill from his pocket. "I figure it must be lucky."

Their architect father helped his students design phenomenal low-cost homes using recycled materials for people without much money. Their mom, an elementary school principal, had dozens of happy jackets and printed scarves in her closet. She remembered every kid's name after the first week of school. If a kid acted up, she said patiently, "Let's get to the bottom of this and see what might help."

"Great parents," Sam and Adrienne said to each other, and they meant it. They had no problems at home. But Adrienne was slightly jealous of her brother.

His affection for unusual information fascinated her. For example, he loved peculiar place names—Bug Tussle on an ancient sign, or Derryfubble Road in Ireland—and he wore T-shirts from Berlin advertising cultural events they had not attended. She didn't even know where he got them. When she asked, he shrugged. On his desk was a pad with two words scrawled on it—Chickahominy Creek.

Adrienne's own interests seemed tame compared to Sam's. Gymnastics. Flute. Traditional American folk songs. No one ever got too excited about them. So she worked to collect details that might intrigue. "We found out about Grandpa's coat while you were gone."

This minor mystery, moth-eaten, with a scrappy collar and an elegant tag, "Montreal Fur Company," had been hanging in their coat closet since Grandpa died last year, arctic in its formidable silence. Grandpa had been one hundred when he died—he didn't speak for the last three years of his life. Adrienne announced proudly, "Grandpa taught in Winnipeg."

"Winnipeg?"

Their Gramps, who scraped by in a rough industrial neighborhood of Mobile, Alabama, who worked in a paper bag factory, who never mentioned Canada or left the state since Sam and Adrienne were born, once lived in Winnipeg? Adrienne had felt snow and ice in his silences, but never chaotic classrooms of rosy-cheeked seventh graders, or horses and sleighs.

"Why wouldn't he tell us that?" Sam marveled. "That old rascal. How did Mom find out?"

"She found some old letters," Adrienne said. "Return address, Winnipeg. He wrote them to Grandma before they married. He described his students in very funny detail. One carried hot sweet potatoes in his pockets. Isn't it weird Gramps wouldn't mention this to Mom, since she's in education, too? Why would he hide it? And why would he go from teaching school to working in a factory? What happened to him?"

Sam shook his head. So many delicious mysteries. Why that mound in the grass? Whose engraved cuff links in the broken box? Why their neighbor Eustacia wouldn't go out on the street during daytime like a normal person? Where Muffy the dog was for six years—before turning up a thousand miles from her home? It was in the paper.

Sam had hidden two hundred dollars last summer, in a

hidden locked cabinet in their bathroom. He was the only one who knew where the key was. The money was saved from his summer job at the plant nursery—he wished he had saved a bit more. With all the talk about failing banks, he didn't want to put it in a bank. He didn't want a bank card, either. People got mugged using bank machines.

"Yes," their mom said. "And people get mugged carrying cash, too."

One day when Sam went to get some of his money, it was gone. Entirely. Even the envelope he had saved it in.

He accused Adrienne, though she never stole things.

"Why would I take it? What do I buy?" She had thought Toys "R" Us was a museum till she was ten.

But no one else . . . maybe she'd found the key and was just tricking him.

Sam finally apologized to her. He told her he checked the cabinet occasionally to see if the envelope might come back. He watched for clues. This made him sound as if he'd read a lot of Nancy Drew. None of the other things in the cabinet had ever gone missing—Grandpa's stamp collection and the mint coin sets encased in plastic.

When Sam went to the cabinet to store the envelope with the dollar bill from his father's ceremony, he had a shock.

He found a solid gold fifty-cent piece, a hundred years

old, overlaid with a gold border, presented as a pendant on a golden chain. It was fancy and heavy and if you wore it on your neck, you would look very ostentatious. Also you would get mugged for sure.

What? Gold coins don't just show up. Neither of his parents had ever seen it before. Adrienne was speechless. What in the world?

"It's as crazy as your money disappearing," she said. "So what do you think *now*?"

Sam looked it up on eBay—similar items had thousand-dollar price tags.

"Maybe ghosts have their own style of banking," Adrienne said. They'd thought there might be a ghost in their bathroom when they were little. The door was always creaking and the water switching on.

Mom turned it over and over in her hands. "I declare," she said. Something her father used to say. "First those Canadian letters stuck in my underwear drawer, now this."

Sam said, "What?"

"Grandpa," Mom said.

We Like You for Your Flaws

On a block of upscale, finely landscaped homes in the Alamo Heights neighborhood, one house stood out—sleekly modern, pale green minimalist, no curtains at any windows, and a front door that could have been designed by an astronaut—matte silver, studded with planetary bumps.

It had been for sale a moment only before the Sold sign was slapped across the realtor's name.

Someone had really wanted that house. The architect who built it was moving to New Zealand.

Jenna and Brianna, who lived across the street in a regular house with a front porch and geranium pots, and liked to lie on their stomachs at night in their twin beds, staring out the window, felt fascinated. Lucky people. No one would buy their house that fast. "If they have a kid, I hope it's a boy," muttered Jenna.

Brianna sighed. "It won't be. It never is. Whatever you want, it's always the other thing."

Their parents had called them the yin and yang twins for years, one positive, one negative, one blond, one brunette. They were really a year apart, but preferred sleeping in the same room so they could exchange secrets late at night, gossip and predict, criticize and fantasize. Talking was their shared talent. They arranged what would have been their other bedroom like a sitting room for teens—TV, game table, couch. They kept that room neat, and their sleeping room messy. It had worked out for them. They were concerned about splitting up when they went to college.

Usually CNN stayed turned on all night in the other room, on mute, with the word-band traveling across the bottom of the screen, collecting bad news from around the world so when they woke in the morning, bleary-eyed, wishing for just another hour of sleep, the one who wasn't in the bathroom yet would stand in the sitting room announcing, "Earthquake! Bombs in Kabul! William and Kate have set the date!"

They saw their new neighbor the day she moved in. She stood in the front yard, long auburn hair streaming loosely across her shoulders. She was staring at her own new house with a pensive look, and appeared to be fifteen or sixteen.

She had a backpack in one hand and an oversize orange purse on her shoulder.

"She should get a different purse," muttered Jenna. "Clashes on her hair."

"Anyway, who needs a purse if you have a backpack?" said Brianna.

A woman came out of the house and drove her off in a black SUV with one dent in the backside.

"Bad day for her," said Jenna. "Meeting all those people at school. Overwhelming."

"How do you know she didn't move here from five blocks away?"

"Did she look comfortable?"

"No."

Because they went to St. Mary's Hall, a private school on the north edge of town, Jenna and Brianna didn't know everyone at the public Alamo Heights High School nearby. But there she was again, their new neighbor, at St. Mary's Hall, standing outside the front office with that purse. She wasn't wearing her uniform yet, which was why they hadn't pegged her.

Jenna walked up to her. "We saw you this morning," she said. "We live across the street."

"Oh," she said. "Hi."

"What's your name?"

The new girl had an inch-long straight scar under her left eye, as if she'd been bitten by a dog in a small town without a good plastic surgeon.

"It's Lily," she said, almost whispering. Brianna noticed it first—her beige shirt was buttoned wrong.

"Where did you move here from?"

"San Angelo. My dad's an art professor. He got a job at the university here. My mom's a sculptor."

Jenna said, "San Angelo?"

"It's really nice, but I'm glad to come to a bigger city," Lily whispered.

"Nice?" they said in unison. How could a place that remote be nice? Where was it, anyway? Lily was nodding.

"What did you like about it?" asked Brianna.

"The people," Lily whispered. "The sunsets. And the lily pad garden."

Jenna and Brianna looked at each other. There was nothing to say to that. And considering her name . . . "We like your house," Jenna said.

"My parents loved it. Because my father's aunt died recently—and he was her only family—we were able to buy it when he got the job here," Lily said.

Jenna stared at Brianna. Money? No one they knew ever talked about money.

"Well, see you around," Jenna said.

"Let us know if you have any questions," added Brianna. But they didn't mean it. Would they tell her their hard-won secrets, who was generous or flighty, which teacher insisted on homework on time and which one didn't?

A week later, after they'd reluctantly dined twice with Lily in the lunch room, invited her over to play Banana-grams in their sitting room, and asked if she wanted to go to the movies on teacher work day (she was going shopping for furniture with her mom)—they wrote her a letter. A combined welcome and apology letter. Jenna wrote the first draft on the computer, then Brianna edited it, then they printed it up on some leftover Valentine paper, with pale pink hearts floating across the top of the page.

"We did not plan to like you," the letter said. "Because your house is so beautiful. Sorry it sounds weird, but it's true. We have a regular house and thought you would be too cool. But after we met you, and discovered you were just like the rest of us, with plenty of flaws—your shirt buttoned wrong on the first day, your voice which is a little too soft, your hair which could use a trim*—we like you after all. If you're interested in going to the Battle of Flowers parade, just let us know."

*They did not mention the scar or the strange slurping sound Lily made when she drank milk.

Killer Chili

Jack was a really bad name to have if you were fat.

Though most people had forgotten all about childhood nursery rhymes, they seemed to remember the one about Jack Sprat eating no fat. They snickered it behind Jack's back—the whispers were stinging.

Jack bussed tables at Riddles Penultimate Cafe on Delmar Boulevard in St. Louis. Sometimes he chopped and stirred, too. Farmers supplying fresh local fruits and vegetables were mentioned by name on the menu—Featuring Green Beans from Mueller's Organic Farm! Sometimes Riddle's served Homemade Ice Cream with Mueller's Organic Blackberries!!!

Joe Mueller, Jack's dad, was thin as a stalk of rhubarb.

His mom Marge was skinny as two strands of whole-wheat spaghetti.

Jack was adopted. Marge and Joe had also adopted fourteen ratty cats and four unattractive dogs. All thin. Everyone in the family was thin but Jack.

"I'll never have romance," he mourned to Rachel, who cooked at Riddle's. "But guess what? I don't care. I just want a few more friends as nice as you."

She assured him, "You're a beautiful man, Jack."

It was the first time he had ever been called a man.

True, he had radiant blossomy skin without a blemish or acne scar. Rachel marveled, "Have you ever had a pimple?"

Jack said, "The least of my worries." He had thick brown hair, perfect teeth.

And he was giving the grapefruit diet one more try. Eat a whole grapefruit fifteen minutes before every meal.

He'd tried the apple cider vinegar in water diet a few months ago, also the diet that said, Eat anything you want for any meal, but only one thing. That could be—one bowl of oatmeal, one piece of toast, one egg—but not all three of them together. And nothing in between. It was pretty rough. Someone mentioned the Mexican food diet—eat as much as you want, but you have to eat it *cold*. So far Jack had been able to lose twelve to twenty pounds quite regularly on any diet he tried, but he always regained it quickly after quitting the diet. He couldn't understand why, since bussing tables involved constant moving around.

"You need a trainer," Rachel said.

"Sure, with all my extra cash."

"Maybe your dad could trade fruits and vegetables with a trainer. Trainers care about eating healthy."

"Well, if you see a hungry trainer, send him my way. You are so lucky to be perfectly *proportioned*."

Rachel laughed. "I love you, Jack."

One Saturday they rode the train downtown to the Arch before starting their evening shift. Shot to the top in the crazy rocket elevator, which neither of them had done since they were little, then sat by the Mississippi to observe old riverboats passing in the languid flow.

"Let's go to New Orleans," Jack said. "We could stow away. . . ." They were wearing their old man hats imprinted with fish that they'd found at the thrift store.

Rachel said, "Did you see the new menu? I don't like it. Too slick. Not our old style. I don't like having the word *Killer* on it."

"What?"

"Killer Brownies, Killer Chili, very negative vibe. I also hate the term *to die for*—who wants to die for a piece of chocolate cake?"

"I agree. It's ugly. Did you tell the boss?"

"That's what I was getting at. Maybe we could talk to him together. Call it Restorer Chili or Comfort Brownies or something—Killer doesn't do it right."

Jack sighed. So many things. He did not support weapons, dead civilians, or young persons led astray into war. So what about all those "I support the troops" signs? He supported nurses, cooks, farmers, street sweepers, kindergarten teachers. Sure, he wanted all citizens to be in free full operation in Afghanistan and Egypt and Tunisia and Iraq and anywhere else you could think of, but was it the responsibility of the United States to make it so? He didn't think people in St. Louis even felt truly responsible for people in Columbia, Missouri. So what the heck?

"We'll do it together."

"I hope we don't get fired."

"We won't get fired."

"Dad, I need a trainer," he said to his hardworking farmer father the next morning at breakfast. Joe was eating his gigantic spread of eggs, grits, biscuits, homemade peach preserves . . . and Jack was eating a grapefruit.

"Look at me, Dad. It's not fair. I eat, like, nothing, and remain huge. You eat everything and you're a lollipop stick."

Joe sniffed. "I work hard all day long. Why don't you help me a little more? Can you pull all those flats of strawberries out to the second section today. I got the wheelbarrow repaired. . . ."

"My mysterious biological parents whom I never wish to meet must have been gargantuan."

"Can't say. Never saw 'em."

"Rachel and I went to the Arch yesterday. It's true, we're turning into a country of fatsos. I counted, like, ten overweight in every group of twelve. But that doesn't make me feel better. I need your help, Dad. I need more tests on my thyroid. Remember how that doctor a few years ago said he'd have to keep his eye on me? Where is he?"

"Lotta money, son."

"I'll work more at the restaurant. We're starting to do catering and I already signed to go on some of those jobs—that could help?"

"College, son. You're on the brink of spending more money than you ever saw. And so am I."

"We could sell Grandmother's silver?"

For some reason, his dad wouldn't hear of this. Tarnished silver trays and silver spoons no one ever used were stashed around their bins and barns like ancient treasure. No one got anything out of them.

"Economic downturn, son; no one wants silver."

"Well there's a guy over on Delmar in a little shop, We Buy Silver, right this minute."

His father sighed. His mother was outside with the cats. Jack pinched himself at the waistline. Bigger.

Lightning

Amal walked up to Joe and Rafael in the hallway.

"It would really be nice," she said, "if you could stop making bad comments about my country in class. They are completely irrelevant to the topic and also inaccurate."

"Why did you leave it if you love it so much?" Joe asked.

"I left it because I am a minor and my parents moved to the United States. If your parents moved to Japan, would you stay here?"

"Definitely," Rafael said. "Ain't no way I'm movin' to Japan."

Amal closed her eyes.

Lockers were clanging around them. The hallway smelled of athletic shoes after a steamy run. "She's gone to sleep," said Joe.

Amal spun around without opening her eyes and stepped into English class. They'd been discussing Edgar Allan Poe and no one but Amal seemed to know he had been an authority on mollusks as well as a poet. "The Raven" would probably not have been the poem he wished to be remembered for. Also, she did not believe Poe died of a drug or alcohol overdose, but more likely, of diabetes, which often went undiagnosed in his day.

"How do you *know* these things?" Mandy had asked her.

"I read."

Amal had also been to the Poe Museum in Richmond, Virginia, which changed everything about how you looked at him. He had incredibly graceful handwriting. No drug addict would be able to write that well.

"Amal, you look stunned," said Mrs. Melchor. "Have you been struck by lightning between classes?"

"Yes," she said. "The lightning of ignorance."

Mrs. Melchor raised her eyebrows.

Amal carefully eased into her chair and tried to smile. An art of its own, the rueful smile. This had been her favorite class all year. Mrs. Melchor paid astonishingly particular attention to every student—if someone had a raging headache, for example, by the end of class Mrs. Melchor would have noticed it on her own, without being told. She had a talent, a gift. She knew when people broke up, or even when their parents did. She was an Observer.

Today they were working on their transcendentalism essays in class. Mrs. Melchor made them handwrite their papers, which pleased Amal because she had retained her penmanship skill. It would have pleased Thoreau, too. He might have made them write with pencil. Some of her friends complained bitterly, said they could only use a keyboard now. Their writing looked clumsy and erratic. Back in Lahore, all class papers had been handwritten, though some students had computers at home. Amal liked to make flourishes on the tails of her letters. They looked almost Arabic, graceful as swans at the park.

Joe, in his geometry class, felt a sharp twinge in his side. Appendicitis?

Did that girl do voodoo? Did they have voodoo wherever it was she came from?

He felt a little restless about razzing her. Of course it wasn't her fault, all the bad stuff that was going on in the news, in the world. What did she say her parents were, that time he accused them of living in caves? Scientists. She said they did medical research. Yeah, sure. Maybe if he were having appendicitis, they wouldn't even fix him. She had said he should read newspapers from other countries online to see how the United States was depicted, then he might be less inclined to make stereotypical accusations.

He said, "I don't even read the school newspaper."

She said, "Part of your problem." He didn't have a problem. He had a pain in his side. Goddammit, she really upset him.

Rafael had completely forgotten to do his assignment. Even though it was for Spanish class, the stupidest class ever, since he had spoken Spanish all his life, he had a hard time keeping up with the written part of it, and had failed to translate his Octavio Paz poem into English, or to write a paragraph about the process. And of course, of course, Mrs. Ramirez called on him first. "Rafael, will you read your translation please?" He was fanning through his messy papers as if looking for it. "Uh, I can't find it," he said.

"We'll wait," said Mrs. Ramirez.

He hated her.

She knew.

She knew he didn't have it and she was torturing him in front of the class.

"It was about—the moon," he said. Everyone laughed. Half of them had gotten the moon poem and the other half had been assigned a longer Alberto Blanco poem about words in boats.

"I don't have it," he finally said. He stopped rooting around like an animal and looked straight up at Mrs. Ramirez. Surly style. Try and make me.

"Well, as you know, Rafael, we are counting homework as eighty percent of this class, since you all know I don't like tests and think homework is a better learning tool. So far you are down around the zero percentile, señor, and your forthcoming grade will represent that."

"I already speak Spanish," he said.

"That will not get you an A if you don't participate in the class and do your homework. That will not even get you a C."

He hated women. This morning his mom had said to his dad, "Even Brad Pitt does more chores than you do." How did she know? Women always thought they were so smart.

Reading Thoreau truly felt helpful to Amal. She didn't care that he had lived 150 years before, or never married, or had dubious feelings about travel. He felt like a friend. He helped her steady herself. "I hope you will tell me if anyone is giving you trouble," Mrs. Melchor whispered kindly, leaning down over Amal's desk and staring at her encouragingly.

Amal smiled back. "Thank you. I will." But she knew she might not. The world was full of trouble. It was up to her to deal with it.

Mailbox

When Mr. Langston died at age sixty-eight, Mattie Hedges, age sixteen, sent Mrs. Langston a card.

It had bluebonnets on it—"With Sympathy for Your Loss." Mattie wrote, "Your husband was so nice to me. He was a great man to everybody. I am very sorry," and signed the card. It seemed like the right thing to do.

Mr. Langston directed the church choir. He told Mattie she was the best alto. Though he had retired some years ago from working at a bank, he still dressed every day with a suit and tie as if he were going to work. He combed his thick gray hair straight back, like Alec Baldwin. Even for Thursday choir practice, when everyone else dressed in their pajamas, practically—he liked to be neat.

Young people loved him because he always looked for

their good points. If they were eating pistachios from their pockets during practice, because they had skipped dinner, he defended them. When they felt estranged or disgusted, he'd ask kindly, "You need to talk about anything?" He didn't give advice, either. That was the best part. He just listened and nodded. Almost miraculously, problems lifted. Mattie thought, When I get older, I want to do that too. Be around for other people. No directions or bossy suggestions—just an open ear. Then she thought, I could do that right now. But it didn't seem to work well with people your own age. They wanted advice.

On the day Mr. Langston died, Mattie was stringing YOUTH CELEBRATION! banners from the trees in front of the church. She was wearing a cheery, springy pink dress, feeling pretty for a change. Even a FedEx delivery man said, "Nice dress!"

Why did it matter so much—to get a little compliment now and then?

After she heard Mr. Langston died, she felt guilty about being self-absorbed with her outfit while someone very dear was leaving the earth. It seemed terrible.

He had disappeared from choir practice without a word. No one said, He's sick, he's in the hospital. Why the secrecy? No one knew he'd had leukemia for years, "the quiet kind." The choir tried to sing without a director at his funeral. They made a mess of it. The altos came in too soon.

Mattie and some of her choir friends took chocolate chip cookies to Mrs. Langston at her home a few days after the big meal at the church. In the super-neat living room, Mattie stared at a few pictures of Mr. Langston when he was young. In the army. At their wedding. He looked gangly and awkward. He had looked more handsome old.

Mrs. Langston received many consoling remembrances those first blurred weeks—also corn chowder, apple muffins, half a ham, bunches of yellow mums, and a white geranium. She tried to write a thank you to every person who was kind to her, hoping she hadn't missed anybody, and lined the cards in a shoebox she found in Mr. Langston's closet. It smelled like him, in a fresh man-shoe kind of way. The flood of attention reminded her of when she had retired from teaching school and received fourteen apple paperweights.

A few weeks later, at the Family Dollar store, Mattie saw a thick purple box of cards on sale (from $2.99 to, yes, a dollar) and had an odd thought. Things would be calming down now over at the Langston home. The funeral was over, coffin in the ground. Would Mrs. Langston feel forgotten and lonesome? Would her mailbox be empty now?

Thinking of You.

Cheery Thoughts!

You're on My Mind.
Just a Little Hello!
It was a perfect cut-rate general Hope assortment.
She bought it.

She sent her second card to Mrs. Langston on the following Monday. He had died on a Monday. Monday would be the day.

Later, at Dollar World and Dollar Tree, Mattie found more cut-rate cards. And at the Salvation Army, a complete vintage box from the 1950s with covered wagons. We're on the trail to cheer you up!

At one point Mattie had a drawer with about a hundred cards in it.

Mattie enjoyed picking out stamps too—No flags, she'd tell the clerk. Any more Love stamps? Something cute or cozy? Kittens?

She was seventeen, eighteen, nineteen. She went to college. She got married too young, to a baritone. Sending the cards every Monday became a sturdy thread through her days. She sent them first from her family home in Waco, then from Waxahachie (married), and Tyler (divorced).

Mattie always added a note. Hope you're doing well. We actually had snow and ice here in Tyler! Stay warm!

Mrs. Langston didn't save all the cards. They seemed to be part of a family. She replied about twice a year, as the years went on, at Christmas and Easter, when you had an excuse to talk to people. While writing Mattie's address, she would get a slightly vague look—now, who was this person? Mr. Langston died a very long time ago, Mrs. Langston thought. Why was Mattie doing this? Once she even wondered, Had Mattie's relationship with Mr. Langston been anything out of the ordinary? But that was impossible. He was a devout Baptist who saw his choir members as the children he never had.

After seven years, at the International House of Pancakes where she went every Sunday after church, Mrs. Langston asked her waitress a strange question. "Have you ever sent more than one sympathy card to someone, after their spouse died?" The cards were resting oddly on her mind that day. The waitress said, "Ma'am, I don't send cards," and Mrs. Langston saw her consulting with other waitresses at the refill station, looking in her direction.

Even after years had gone by, and Mattie had honestly forgotten how the tradition started, each Monday she closed her eyes for a little prayer, selected the next card, pulled a stamp off its adhesive backing, and started a new week.

My Gospel

In those days things were still beginning more than ending. A light fog in the morning wrapped the pecan trees and park benches with a softness the rest of the day would not repeat. At seven a.m. the old-fashioned bell from St. Mary's Church echoed through the city. At exactly that moment, Leo picked the newspaper up in his front yard (he needed it with his breakfast), and paused to listen to the bell. There was hope in its clear note. Even if you didn't go to church, you felt it.

Leo's life seemed simple to him. He liked to hear the bell, but he didn't bow to it. So it was hard for him to understand Rainey's complex subtleties, her desire to hide. What was she hiding from? She acted as if things were ending more than beginning. But she was only seventeen, too, so that didn't make much sense.

"Would you like to go to the White Rabbit?" he'd asked her, on the day they met over a dead bird. (It would always be a strange thing to tell people, even twenty years later, when they were married for years already and their little girl stood on her head on a yoga mat in their backyard.)

Rainey stared at him. "What is it?"

"What is it? A music club! You never went there? Exene Cervenka and Dex Romweber Duo are there this Friday, with a mystery guest. It's a crazy place! Wear a coat, though, because sometimes it gets very cold in there."

He might as well have been inviting her to the mineral baths in Budapest, the way she stared at him.

"I don't know if I can."

"What about *Grapes of Wrath*—have you seen it yet?"

Their school play was receiving rave reviews. Even university theater students and people from the community were packing the house. Leo ran the curtain and felt proud—also amazed.

"I'll have to think about it," she said.

Leo subscribed to *Paste* and *Rolling Stone* and *No Depression*. He loved reading about musicians and bands he had never heard of before. Sometimes he would track them down on YouTube or at Hogwild Music store later. The iPod was probably the best invention since the car. He played the saxophone and at *Grapes of Wrath*, offered a single haunting solo between acts. Two girls sang some old Dust Bowl songs after him. Rainey said later, it was that moment, when he came out onstage wearing raggedy gray pants with black suspenders and lifted his shiny sax, when her whole world changed. For him, the moment would remain the dead bird.

His mom thought he had a destiny as a music critic, maybe a producer. She could never have guessed he would someday run the food bank.

Ever since he was small, Leo had wanted to know more about the men and women sleeping under the I-37 bridge, stirring coals and twigs in the lid of an old metal trash can, lining up for new used shoes in the Avenue E parking lot. He wanted them to have everything they needed—food, shelter, security—but also, he wanted them to have more music.

The struggling people of Haiti, after the earthquakes, had been singing in the streets—old gospel songs, hymns. News reporters seemed broken up about this as they described it. But of course, Leo thought. We need music when we're happy but even more when we're sad or confused. Good music lifting us out of our skins. Unexpected symphonies. Put some blues there, under the bridge, and things will feel better.

Leo had heard that street lamp poles in Tokyo played soft music at twilight—he was anxious to travel there to confirm this for himself. (They would go to Japan for their honeymoon. And, it was true. Rainey's eyes blinking madly with tears as a light pole, for god's sake, played an old tune her father had loved.)

Once while Leo was waiting in a hospital as his dad had surgery, he played the same round of songs by Bright Eyes over and over. After that he couldn't play him for a while. But he felt as if Conor Oberst were his personal friend who had gotten him through a lot of worry one day. When Rainey told him she had been heartbroken to learn from nurses at the hospital where her father died that he had played classical music on the remote-control radio in his hands all night before he departed, Leo asked, "Why heartbroken? That's beautiful! Your father knew how to find beauty when he needed it. He was smart."

Shortly after they met, Leo and Rainey went to see an amazing movie, *Me and Orson Welles*. Although Rainey objected softly to the title's grammar, they both adored the film and decided the music of 1937 had a profoundly grounding effect. They came out of the theater and wanted to walk home instead of driving. But what would they do about the car? It was his dad's old Outback. He couldn't just leave it parked at the mall.

She stared at him with amazement. Had she ever met anyone more enthusiastic? His brown hair tumbled over his collar. When he was speaking, his hair bounced. At the same time he was very low-key. Rainey decided she could trust him that evening.

They wished they had long black overcoats and could walk to an old-fashioned diner right then, in the dark, humming.

On Valentine's Day they went to a grocery store together and while she was looking for apples and cheese for their picnic by the river, he was standing near the onions with his eyes closed, tapping his foot, saying, James Taylor mellow oldies in the produce aisle, this is the best, really, makes you feel like no time is wasted, it even makes me hungrier, let's get bananas and walnuts, too.

New Man

Mom, Dad, I think I got baptized.

I don't know what happened really but suddenly someone was throwing me into a pool of water and praying over me and it was really surprising, I mean, I know you will be surprised, too, because I didn't know it was coming.

I shouldn't have been listening to my iPod in the bus. I think they made an announcement that I missed.

When our guys rode over there, I thought we were just going to practice on the other team's field, you know, we had all our gear and we were really tired after school and Coach said he wanted us to hear someone give a talk, I thought like a motivational speaker, after practice, and I put the music on after that and didn't hear anything else he said if he said more, but I think that was all of it. I know, I know. The bus was making a lot of noise with that construction on the highway and we had to detour on the access road a couple of times, it was really bumpy, I closed my eyes and when I opened them, Randy was holding his stomach but he didn't really get sick, it wasn't that bad, I'm sorry, are you mad at me for what I'm telling you?

Of course I saw it was a church when we got there, how could I not see it was a church? Churches are pretty recognizable. It wasn't a big church. It was like one of those back roads churches. Well, I thought the speaker was going to be there. We sat in the pews awhile. No, I didn't listen to the iPod then, of course not. That would definitely be a ticket to demerits, are you kidding?

Coach was up in the front row, I could see the back of his head.

I don't remember anyone asking my opinion about anything, no way, not asking, like, did I want to do it, did I not want to do it, nothing.

It was mostly Bible lessons and the speaker was pretty dramatic, not dead and whiny like some of the preachers I've seen, no offense to either of you, I know you love your preacher and your priest, but face it, they're yours, not mine. I inherited them from you. No way I would have started going to either of your churches if you had given me the choice, I mean that sincerely, I would not just have been walking down the street and stepped into either of your churches and thought, Wow, this is great, I'll come back here.

Why are you crying, Mom?

I mean that very kindly.

You have to respect my own opinion, right? I mean, if I have to respect yours?

Well maybe not, okay. But I had no idea I was going to get thrown into a vat any moment there, seriously, it is not my style, when we got up to walk down the aisle I thought they wanted us to sign something, like a guest book, or to shake hands, like we do with the other team after a game, it was no big deal, no one said, This is going to be a life-changing moment, no, that's not what I mean, I don't feel my life is changed, yes, he talked about rebirth issues, that we were getting born again in Christ, but doesn't everyone always talk about that? It's pretty routine, like a pep talk, isn't it? I mean, do you really get born every time you say "born"—no way. That would be confusing. I mean, you thought you were already happening and you had your legs and body and everything and then you're just a little baby all over again, it would be really tedious. It's just a simile. Or a metaphor. Of course I didn't want to get born again, it's only Monday. We just started school last week. I just found all my seats in class and everything.

What did the preacher say before he dipped us? Well, there were a few people dipping us. We're strong.

Uh, I think he said, Do you really want to listen to the story of Jesus or do you just want to tell your own story?

That seemed kinda strange to me because none of us were talking, know what I mean? Kinda rude.

He said he knew how we felt, that in life it's always hard to know what to do first.

Well, that's true.

But I don't think he knows how I feel. He doesn't even know me. I do not know the guy, no. I have never seen him before in my life.

And, lemme think, he also said, Some days you're just down in the dumps, no two ways about it. Well, that's certainly true. Like now. Like having to tell you I just got baptized as if it were a drive-by or something, very strange. This is really stressing me out.

He said when we're down in the dumps, Jesus is what we need. Which I do think I have heard more than once at both of your churches, no offense but it wasn't like a newsbreak or anything.

And then they threw us in this vat and pressed our faces down, god! I have to admit I kind of shouted it. God! And they thought I was praying. They told me I am a new man. Not only me, all the guys. We're a whole new team I guess. I don't know what the other guys thought, they looked shocked too. We were very quiet in the bus coming back. I think we were all thinking about telling our parents what just happened. And if we were new men would you recognize us? Ha ha ha.

Play Me a Tune

Whatever your life, you developed certain proficiencies. Even something no one else cared about. Secret.

Good at walking swiftly down a block in the dark.

Good at coaxing a dead plant back to life.

Good at feeding a crying cat, making him stand on his hind legs to touch the rim of the stool just once before you plopped the food into his bowl.

Good at putting contacts in, slipping them out.

Good at waxing a car.

Good at hitting a home run in Little League and remembering that cheering forever (nothing else would quite live up to it).

What was Miko's?

He wondered this sometimes—

He was a decent observer.

His room wasn't the messiest in town.

He could make a really good pizza if he bought the crust.

And all those other little things (see above) but nothing was Headline Material. He wasn't winning the science fair.

"I'm doing my best," his dad would say, in a tone that sent chills up Miko's spine. That meant his dad wasn't doing well at all. He could interpret his dad. And his mom, too. No prizes were given for this talent. No one sent you a scholarship because you had managed to negotiate the various depressions of two parents without being bumped too far off course yourself.

As a young boy, with sisters eight and ten years older than he was, everything was easier. He had four parents for the first years of his life. They dressed and redressed him. He wore snazzy stripes and a Greek fisherman's cap with his blond curls sticking out. They took pictures. He was the court jester, the adorable surprise. His mom got him onto a local TV commercial for Art Night.

But then his sisters grew up and left, not only the house, but the country, both of them passionate about speaking French and eating fresh hot croissants and baguettes every day from a bakery by their French art college. His sisters loved each other so much, they were looking for twin boyfriends.

And where did this leave him? A suddenly-only child in lovely, lonely Nebraska with two depressed parents, missing their beautiful girls. The girls had done so much. Cooking, cleaning, cheering everything forward. And now . . .

"I think I might go see the cranes this weekend, some people are going," Miko said at breakfast. He put down his fork. There would be objections.

"What people?" His mom sighed.

"Oh, some guys from band. We'll share a motel room so it doesn't cost too much, or maybe we'll just drive back after sunset."

"Drive in the dark?" his father said, looking up from the newspaper. "It's probably better if you stay over there. Are you going to the Audubon place? I heard they're here in full force, really big year. All that corn in the fields."

"Yeah, we heard that, too."

The massive flocks of gray sandhill cranes settling into the Platte River at sunset were one of the wonders of the Midwestern world. And they only paused in Nebraska for a short time.

"Stay there. Watch the morning liftoff too, then drive back. Don't forget your big coat. And whose car are you taking? Not another car with bad tires please. You want to take the Prius? I'll let you."

"Yeah, sure. I would love to take the Prius. Thanks. We

won't spill food in it this time I promise. Mom, everything okay? You seem really quiet."

"Oh, the usual, I'm doing my best."

His mother suffered painful arthritis. She wouldn't take painkillers, though. One thing you learned with a depressed person, never ask them why they're "sad." Because they're not sad, they're just regular, for them. Also, giving advice was never good because they wouldn't take it. You just gave them something else to resist.

"Dad, what are you doing today?"

His father still worked at the Omaha newspaper. Though many people said newspapers were a dying institution, his father had, by now, filled every single position the newspaper had to offer, except women's advice columnist. And he read the newspaper every morning as if he had never seen it before. Scoured even the ads and obituaries. "Actually I'm going to see Warren Buffett's troop of thirteen-year-old recorder players rehearse—they're doing a concert soon. I'm writing a story about them."

Now that was cool. Warren Buffett had bought all the sleek little recorders in purple felt sacks with drawstrings and was even known to show up for after-school practices. He had loved playing a recorder as a child himself. And he wanted to share it.

Miko and his parents actually lived in Warren Buffett's modest brick neighborhood and were so impressed that the super-billionaire hero of their state and country had never moved away. He could have lived in a much bigger house with high security and glorious meadows and horse barns. He could have lived in a castle on a seacoast. He could have had butlers and secret gardens and anything he wanted. But he chose to buy recorders for kids.

Miko filed this in his mental cabinet:

Heartwarming Stories. Stories you could tell a downbeat person in a bad moment.

You had to collect those things.

The person who gives away half of what he has.

The ladies building water tanks and reading rooms in small African towns.

Mysteries of crane migration—without Google maps or radar screens—had been maintained for centuries—clear passage through the skies, for thousands of miles. No matter what mistakes people made on earth, they showed up. When they cried, your deepest memory echoed. They carried nothing for their journey, but the corn plumping their flesh, under their feathers.

Now that was traveling light.

Miko didn't know how he felt about God or his own future. When asked for college plans, his mind went blank as snow. But he knew how he felt about looking up sometimes, and staying quiet.

Second Thoughts
Are the Only Thoughts
I Have

Because I didn't just get here, Rainey thought.

Only if you recently arrived on earth could you be having first thoughts.

Replay, rewind. . . .

Try the sock store in Cairo.

How many times had she thought about it by now?

The small unobtrusive store was located in a long shopping hallway off the lobby of the Nile Hilton, near Tahrir Square, where she and her father stayed for seven days of the Christmas holiday. Since it was Egypt, of course, Christmas was also unobtrusive. Which was fine with Rainey. Her parents had pointed out to her long ago that the baby Jesus lying in a manger might really dislike those newspaper ads.

LAST DAY TO SHOP! 40% DISCOUNT ADDED TO 30% DISCOUNT!

And that truly stupid question people always asked around the holidays in the United States, Are you ready for Christmas? which basically meant, Have you shopped? Rainey's mom would answer, "I will never be ready for Christmas in a world of war."

Other stores on the hotel's shopping hall sold goat soap, expensive facial potions, glittering designer party dresses, Egyptian curios, but the sock store stood out. "I wonder how much business they do," her father mused. "I guess a lot of people must forget their socks when they travel. Actually, I need to go there. Somehow I packed only one extra pair of socks in my luggage. Don't know what I was thinking. Maybe they were all in the wash." On a mysterious holiday business trip for his company, for which he would be paid overtime, he was attending secretive meetings four times a day and Rainey was visiting mummified remains of ancient pharaohs, writing esoteric details in a black notebook.

In the evenings Rainey and her father would walk out to the riverfront where glittering gambling boats broadcast enticing music. They would stroll up and down like in the old days, watching the sun sink, the Nile turn pinkish golden for a few moments, and the swallows diving toward the water. "I always loved Cairo," her father sighed. "We could have lived here. Why didn't we?"

They would walk to Café Riche where black-and-white

portraits of local writers and intellectuals hung on all the walls, including the great novelist Naguib Mahfouz—people who had eaten there. So when you ordered rice, you were part of a long stream of people ordering rice for a hundred years. Second thoughts? Lentil soup, steaming warm brown bowl with a little dab of yogurt on top, like a snowdrift. "Dad, how many bowls of lentil soup do you suppose one person eats in a lifetime?"

He said what he always said, which had never made sense, "We would have to ask the queen."

That morning Rainey had been halfheartedly watching BBC TV when Queen Elizabeth remarked in her annual address to the nation, "Some years are best forgotten."

Rainey asked her dad, "Do you think that is true?"

He said, "No. The queen is sometimes wrong. And some people never eat lentil soup at all."

"We should remember all our years?"

"Yes, because in the full picture, we don't get many of them. So giving up a whole year would be a big loss."

Rainey would never have believed her father would be dead three months later. He was a vital, vigorous man, fluent in three languages, funny and confident. They talked about petty things. She rolled her eyes. She said, "How are your socks doing?"

"Terrible. We have three more days here. I really have to

get down to that store." But the store was always closed by the time he got back to the hotel for their late dinner.

So the next day, she visited the sock store while he was gone, to surprise him with a present when he returned. It was Christmas, after all.

She stepped through the door and three attendants pounced on her. It was as if she were the first person to enter in years. One spoke in Arabic, one in French, and one in English. Her dad would have felt right at home—all three of his languages, spoken simultaneously.

"Umm—socks," Rainey said.

But of course. What else, lemons?

A pair of sleek olive green socks caught her eye, mostly because a pair of mannequin feet next to the cash register was wearing them.

She pointed at them and smiled. How would her father feel about green socks? Maybe he would like them for the holiday season. He wasn't big on flamboyant garb. Yesterday when they'd seen a man in the lobby wearing a red-checkered jacket, her dad had said, "Ouch."

Two of the sock people opened a sock box and pulled out a stack of the green socks. They were very smooth. They were also expensive. What were they, cashmere? Rainey nodded. She could afford one other pair plus the fancy green, with the bills she had in her pocket.

She stared into the eyes of the three people in front of her. How on earth could this empty store afford so many clerks? And why did they seem so earnest—about men's socks? Couldn't they branch out and sell . . . women's socks, too? Fancy hosiery?

The three clerks seemed so hopeful, she could have cried. They wanted her to buy a hundred pairs of socks. They wanted to serve her well. They folded the socks in reams of fragrant tissue. Her father grimaced only briefly when she presented the green socks at dinner. He tried to feign enthusiasm. Did he ever, ever wear them? They seemed really fresh when she found them later in his drawer at home. Still with their little Arabic cotton tag. He wore the black ones, though. She wanted him to enjoy everything. Like the pyramid builders of ancient times, focused on their beloved kings, she wanted him to live forever.

Mary Alvarez Is Ninety Today

My family always finishes my milk. Which is why you will frequently find me jogging to the grocery store at six-thirty a.m. to replenish the refrigerator, as if I am the servant for the house. You are, they say, the one so desperate for lactose-free double-protein milk. So go and get it. But why does everyone else guzzle it? That's what I want to know.

I buy two every time at $2.99 each. I can't really jog home so I walk briskly with one in each hand. I drink one half gallon a day. That's a lot of milk money. Then they drink half of the second one when my back is turned.

I am frequently in a bad mood at the grocery store. It is not really where I want to be first thing every day, but I can't eat breakfast without milk and I can't live without breakfast.

So marry a cow, my brother says.

Marry a grocer, bring back the milkman industry, go to hell why don't you.

He pretends he has the same lactose intolerance as our Arab father but this milk, being lactose-free, doesn't bother him.

So today when I'm in a really grouchy mood waiting at the checkout, there's this old guy with a ponytail behind me buying a heart-shaped balloon. It's 6:48 a.m. and I can't help myself. "Must be true love!" I say.

Instantly I feel rude but he looks up from unloading tangerines and frozen lasagna boxes from his cart and says, "Oh, hi," as if we know each other. Then, "It's for my mom." My first thought is, He looks old to have a mom, but I try to hold my eyebrows down.

He says, "It's her birthday. She's ninety today."

Then I start doing the math. He could be sixty-eight, sixty-nine.

"Wow," I say. "Happy birthday to her."

He says, "I guess you're an early bird? So am I."

I say, "Actually, I am someone desperate for milk. My family keeps drinking mine."

He grins at me.

"What is your mother's name?" I say.

"Mary Alvarez."

He says it so proudly, as if she's a saint or a mayor.

"Well, have a beautiful day, Mary Alvarez, we wish you many more," I say, punching the air, and he smiles very kindly and says, "Thank you so much."

So Mary, I think, walking home with my milks, how has it been, celebrating your birth all these years the same day as Día de los Muertos, when people remember the dead? Coming and going. That's all we do in this world. Buy the milk and drink the milk. Strengthen the bones, then die.

My mom didn't make a shrine this year. We made one at school, with Michael Jackson on it, and our old janitor Mr. Diaz, the nicest guy on the face of the earth, and a lot of personal relatives of different people, but for some reason I didn't want to participate, though I was seriously tempted to bring a picture of my dog. I just didn't want anyone to laugh. He was such a great dog.

Have a good day, Mary. Have a beautiful day. I look both ways crossing St. Mary's and even think of you inside the old street name, swinging my plastic bags of milk. Maybe I could hide the cartons in the refrigerator's vegetable bin under the lettuce and carrots. It's strange but I decide to act less grouchy in the mornings from now on as a present to you. A person I will never meet. You have a nice son. Does his ponytail ever bug you?

See How This Thing Goes

"Why didn't you call me?"

Jane couldn't believe she was staring at Tessa in a hospital bed.

Tessa's voice, thinned and faint. "Because if you knew, it would make it more real. I don't want it to be real."

"It is not real!"

Tessa turned her face to the side, into the giant white pillow.

How could it be real?

Normally Jane didn't see Tessa during summers. Tessa went to her grandparents' in Virginia, where her horse lived, and Jane stayed home to babysit the neighbor kids, and labor long hours at Melt, the ice cream store owned by her weird, weird cousin.

This year in July, Jane received a message from their friend Sam, working at Disney World in Florida. He was not impersonating Minnie Mouse, as usual. "That's horrible, about Tessa. Call and tell me what you know."

She knew nothing. Had Tessa been thrown by a horse?

She called Tessa's mom. Jane had heard about the Christopher Reeve accident when she was little and it scared her. Horses were elegant moving gracefully far off in a field, but Jane had no desire to sit on one. Tessa had been riding horses all her life. The idea of spending an entire equestrian summer galloping and jumping around meadows seemed strange to Jane.

Tessa's mother finally called back. "Go see her at Methodist; I'm up there most of the time. She fainted while riding and fell off her horse—we are very lucky she didn't break her neck or back. They're doing tests, but right now it looks like a tumor that may not be operable."

"What does that mean?"

There was a big silence.

Jane thought about the body, its mysterious hallways and little banging doors. All her life she'd considered how her heart, her very best friend, was completely unseen to her, chugging away, doing its duty, keeping everything else going, but invisible. No applause. When you were well, scooping ice cream into an endless stream of sugar cones for whiny kids, you didn't think about the heart. You thought about the wrist, how much it hurt when you went home. You wore one of those tight bands like tennis players wear, to make it feel better. But the heart, the kidneys, the liver, the arteries and veins, they were sort of on their own.

You did not worry about tumors showing up.

You did not worry about suddenly falling off an escalator or into a pond.

You did not worry about the heart hanging up its small white towel and saying, I've had enough of this. After long days at work, Jane often thought, This is not my store. I could do something else. If everything really did *melt*, it wouldn't matter to me.

"You will get well!" Jane said, sitting close to Tessa's bed, twirling her friend's long brown hair around one of her own fingers against the pillow. "They'll do something! You will! You have to!"

"I want to," Tessa whispered. "We just have to see how this thing goes."

In the hallway outside Tessa's room, a huge heart monitor or regulating device was being delivered, its head covered in a plastic bag. The men pushing it laughed and joked about it having a mind of its own. It was hard to turn it through the door and park it at the foot of Tessa's bed. Probably they didn't have any friend or relative sick in the hospital right that minute.

Jane didn't like how Tessa was talking—as if "the thing" were in charge, not her.

"What did the horse do when you fell off?" Jane said. Tessa was not chatting much, so she kept asking things.

"Well, another rider nearby told me it came back and looked at me," Tessa said. "Leaned over into my face and stared. It was really good my foot didn't get caught in the stirrup."

When they were younger, Tessa had once told Jane, "I feel closer to animals than to people," which hurt Jane's feelings. Jane had wished she could say, "So do I," especially when people let her down, like right that minute, but even her cat scratched her.

The door to the room opened again and Tessa's mom entered with tomato bisque soup and sour cream muffins, their favorite foods. But Jane didn't want any. "C'mon, you've had lunch with us a hundred times!" How could she be so cheery? Maybe she was just good at covering up. She was wearing a necklace.

Tessa said she'd try. A few bites. Tessa's mom was winking at Jane like, Be a sport.

Jane peeled the paper off a muffin for Tessa. She arranged it on the side table where Get Well cards were stacked next to a Kleenex box. The cart had wheels. Everything here had wheels.

Jane poured a little soup into the top of a thermos. It was still steaming.

Tessa said, "Feed me," and grinned devilishly.

Jane picked up a spoon, then paused. Did she mean it?

Tessa had fed the horse some carrots and apples that morning she fell. Noticed how his jaws opened so elegantly, how he took the carrots between his teeth and bit clean through. One moment the world was your friend. You knew where you stood, what happened next. The horse understood the feel of the ground beneath him, the meadow when it was muddy, or drier and dusty, the screech of the gate every morning when Tessa walked through. He liked her hand on his neck, scratching beneath the mane, he liked pleasing her, galloping back toward the barn with the slightest of nudges. What he didn't understand was the day she was lying on the ground, the sudden lightness, how she didn't speak to him then, or press him with her knees, or pull a rein either way, and when he looked into her face, the stillness. He lifted his head into the wind and the wind was cool and he waited.

See You in Ireland

Liyana heard Omer was in jail by accident.

She was back in St. Louis with her parents and brother, visiting their grandmother, Peachy Helen, who'd had a mysterious collapse. Liyana read an e-mail from their friend Khaled, sent to her brother Rafik, and copied to her.

It was so strange how news traveled these days. You could kick a stone on a sidewalk and find a little message to yourself tucked under it.

She ran into the next room where Rafik was drowsing on Peachy's old mustard-colored nubby couch.

"What?" she said. "Hurry, get up!"

He hadn't read the message yet, so had no idea.

"Did she die?"

"Come read this message—tell me what it means!"

Rafik looked surprised in his sleepiness. Liyana rarely asked him to explain anything. He staggered into the dining room, where Poppy's laptop was set up on Peachy's floral placemat, collecting all their messages from across the sea in its hardworking stomach.

He blinked.

"Why are you reading my e-mail?" he asked.

"I'm not! This was copied to me! But go into your own messages and find out more if you can!"

Their parents were at the hospital. Peachy was having another CAT scan. She thought she'd had a heart attack or a stroke, but the doctors couldn't find anything.

Liyana and Rafik, left alone in Peachy's familiar lavender bath oil fragrance, had time to transport back to early childhood, before they ever left for Jerusalem, and she used to let them scissor newspapers all over her floor, never once saying, "Clean it up." Liyana thought there might be shreds of paper still stuffed under the bed.

She felt sad looking around at Peachy's rooms—their fatso baby pictures, faded drawings tacked to her walls. Peachy had been brave enough to fly across the ocean and visit them once—she said she could never do it again.

It was strange to be back in the States and not feel close to their old St. Louis neighborhood. Two and a half years since they were last here, but it felt longer. No one missed them anymore. They were scraps of old weather reports tucked under the dresser.

And there was too much traffic now, too many people with tattoos. What was up with that? Everything seemed a bit off-kilter.

Rafik read his own messages slowly, then shook his head.

"I guess you know now why Omer hasn't been writing you. Khaled says a *bunch* of people went to jail. Everything is crazy."

They'd been gone five days. Liyana hadn't heard from Omer once. Very unlike him.

"Is he your boyfriend?" Rafik asked again, staring at her hard, and she said, "Bigger. You know that."

Before they left Jerusalem, demonstrations had been heating up in all directions. Circus performers balancing along the top of the wall had been arrested. A boy was jailed for flying a kite. At least more people were advocating on one another's behalf these days, everyone wearing keffiyehs so you could hardly tell who was who. Even a Norwegian was arrested—someone thought he was an Arab. So many people saying, Let's improve these problems right now! Except extremists. Extremists never wanted things to improve. They just wanted to win. They needed psychiatrists.

"Who can we call?"

"Could you call his house?"

But Omer's mother didn't speak English, only Hebrew.

"I could call Khaled's cell, right? How much would it cost?"

"Poppy said we weren't supposed to make calls overseas while we are here, remember?" Their Arab father was very . . . thrifty.

"Yeah, but this could be an emergency."

"Why not just send an e-mail?"

So Liyana wrote back to Khaled.

"Why is Omer in jail? Did you see him? Can you take him a message from me?"

Rafik asked, "What is the message?"

"None of your business."

Maybe the message would be, Break out. Whatever it takes, get out of there. And what kind of jail—Israeli? Palestinian? She didn't know which one was worse.

Maybe, Let's run away to Ireland and set up a shop selling Arab and Jewish treats. I'll speak my pedestrian Arabic and you speak Hebrew and our shop will be papered with peace signs and we'll get married when we're twenty-seven. We won't call it Holy Land Desserts though. The words *Holy Land* don't seem to help.

Maybe, I love you, stay safe!

Khaled wrote back right away. It was incredible how much time he spent sitting in the computer room at the

refugee camp where he still lived. He liked to go there at two
a.m. when his neighbors were sleeping. More privacy that
way.

"He made your quote on his sign. They say he crossed
a line, or broke rule—he now in Israel jail. *Ha!* Jewish boy
in Israel jail. Everyone talking about it. His mom making
hunger strike in front of jail, also she kick a soldier."

Well, of course. She would. His mama loved her boy.
Everyone loved their boys and girls. Wasn't that reason
enough to make peace? But his mama also loved to eat, so
the hunger part was hard to believe. . . .

Liyana pushed Rafik off the chair and pecked out,
"What quote?"

Rafik said, "That's selfish! You care more about your
quote than Omer?"

"Of course not. I'm curious. What quote of mine could
get someone arrested?"

Khaled wrote back, "Don't know."

She pecked, "What can we do from here?"

It could have been anything.

She closed her eyes and sighed. She'd just remembered
the one he liked. Because he rejected "the chosen people"
idea so strongly. But jail?

DEAREST JEWS, PLEASE CHOOSE TO BE NICER.

Something He Left Me

San Marcos, Texas, was not a very big city. So surely, Erin thought, she would be able to find her father when she got there. Though his name had not appeared on the Switchboard.com site when she checked it, and his old numbers were disconnected, she felt certain she could stick her nose into a coffee shop or hardware store, and discover him.

Follow the clattering truck.

Follow the men with hammers.

She'd find him building something.

She'd find him drinking a Coors down by the old gas station turned into a music club.

"Don't do it," her mother had said to her a few months ago, when Erin mentioned she might stop by San Marcos on her way to Austin. "You're just setting yourself up for pain and anguish if you do something like that."

But pain and anguish were everywhere anyway. Might as well put them to good use.

Erin knew a guy, Sam, from San Marcos—they'd gone to tennis camp outside Corpus Christi together one summer. He'd said she could sleep on his couch if she ever needed to. "Or, I'll give you the bed and take the couch. You can use all three of my spoons, too." But somehow she didn't want to call him unless she had to spend more than one day. She had the crazy idea she could find her dad in two hours.

San Marcos seemed sweet. Not at all an ominous town. There was a nice library and a drive-thru beer barn. Maybe Erin should just sit in the entry lane and wait.

"He might not be going by Rusty anymore," her mom had mentioned. "He said he wanted to go back to Pete." Rusty had been stuck on him by other people, the old red hair thing. He never liked it.

"I didn't really know my dad," Erin always said, when her friends asked about him. "I was so little when he left. I remember his laugh and the way he lifted me up and twirled me high in the air. But I guess all dads do that."

"They do not," said Genine.

Erin's mom had disappointed her by never dating anyone after Rusty/Pete left, except for a few outings with the

Fried Oysters man who smelled like breading and grease. Her mom was cute, too. She said to Erin, "I need to focus on *you*."

This was a problem.

Erin said, "Please, I want to go to college *alone*. Let me unpack and organize my own room. You'll try to make the bed or something. You come up to Austin and visit me later, okay?"

Her mother's lip trembled and Erin felt terrible. But it had to be said.

She'd had practice being independent—every day after school, after tennis—coming home to an empty house, unlocking the door, having Molly the dog jump on her and lick her, be her best companion.

That part would be hard in Austin. No Molly.

Why did Erin think a simple sit-down conversation with the man who had shadowed her whole life would be helpful, in terms of clearing the air?

You totally disappointed me.

We were always waiting and secretly hoping.

Every time the doorbell rang.

Mom is still kinda a wreck, you know.

And couldn't you at least have visited once a year on my birthday or something, would that have been so hard?

Could you just comment on my dimples once please?

Mom doesn't have them.

I don't care if you were never married, you are still my dad.

She got out of her little golden Kia near the town square. The trunk and backseat were stuffed with luggage—her computer, the giant fluffy teddy bear she could not leave at home . . . so she was a little worried about walking out of sight of the car. She didn't want to get robbed.

"Excuse me, do you know Mr. Rusty Fincher?" Erin spoke to men in bandannas cracking a street wide open. They stared at her blankly.

"Hey, is Rusty Fincher up there with you?" she shouted to men on scaffoldings on a tall white church.

She drifted around, glancing back at her parking space frequently. She walked out of sight of the car for a few blocks. She looked down at her own feet. Pedicure, new sandals. Start off college right. Don't go partying every night like some of the people she knew in high school.

"Excuse me," she said to a man in a GET DOWN! T-shirt at a crosswalk. "You wouldn't happen to know a Rusty or Pete Fincher, would you? Red ponytail, probably?"

He stared at her. "Both of 'em? Two guys with red ponytails?"

"No, one guy with two names."

"I do not."

She asked the waitress pouring coffee at the Little Bucket. She stared into the window of a falafel joint. Someone was mopping the floor in there. He was not her father. She asked the man getting into the next car back on the square. Then she dialed Sam's number and left a message. Hey, just passing through, moving to Austin today! Check in with me and maybe we can get together some weekend soon.

Okay, she thought. I give up. For today. She drove around the rim of the San Marcos university campus, then down to a creek where she parked a few minutes. Maybe it was a river, not a creek. Hard to tell in Texas sometimes. Bodies of water narrowed and widened unpredictably. Ducks were curled up beside the stream as if guarding their eggs. They seemed to be in couples, too. Girl ducks with guy ducks, side by side.

What did she want from him?

Good job, Erin.

You made it through with no help from me.

Your mom did a real good job, too.

She was a looker back when.

I'm proud of you though I have no right to be.

I'm sorry.

Teeth

Steven never dreamed his cat would come back after a year and attack him. It was like a horror movie. Your mom sends you out to drag the massive trash can on wheels to the street and a snarling mound of dirty gray fur leaps out of the windowsill next to the can and sinks its longest teeth into the vein in your wrist. Quite unexpected.

The blood spurted like a fountain all over the fresh striped blue-and-white shirt he was wearing to school. His mom tied a clean rag around his arm, pirate style. They went to the emergency clinic, leaving his hot scrambled eggs on the table.

The doc cleaned up the wound, put a few stitches in.

Steven hadn't had a tetanus shot in ten years, so Doc said he needed a new one. Kind of embarrassing—I was attacked by my old cat Jesse. The dude looked really bad.

What the heck? Jesse used to sleep on the foot of his bed.

The doc asked, "Did he ever attack you before?"

"Never!"

When Jesse disappeared on that rare day of snow last year, first snow in south Texas in thirteen years, Steven's parents thought the cat had become disoriented, been picked up by someone who felt sorry for him, and carted off to a new home. He was a good-looking cat. Steven and his parents had tacked posters on telephone poles but never gotten a call. Maybe Jesse had been trying since then to escape and return home to them. Maybe he blamed them for not rescuing him.

Most importantly, where was Jesse now? The doctor said he had to be captured and kept at the pound under observation for rabies for thirty days. Great. So now Steven had to start looking for him again? If you don't find him, the doctor said, I'd recommend you get rabies shots anyway. Right there, boom, in your stomach. Since the cat was acting uncharacteristic, he might well be sick. Terrific news. It was not the best morning.

Steven didn't get to school till ten-thirty and missed the quiz on J. D. Salinger. He wished he liked Salinger's books better. Everyone was staring at his bandaged wrist. "No, I did not try that," he said. Somehow it fit with Salinger. He wished Salinger had come out of seclusion before he died. It seemed a waste not to tell people, directly, about some of the things going through his mind for all those years. Especially when he didn't mind telling them early on.

After school Steven's mom said he needed to crawl under the house to look for the cat.

"Mom! What if he jumps on my head? Seriously!"

"Well, speak softly, see if you can locate him. Jesse knew you best. That's where he always went, remember? Once you spot where he's hiding, we'll call Animal Control to come out with nets. The doctor said it's important we find him today. And don't get your wound dirty!" She gave him a plastic bag to tie around his arm.

He almost wished Jesse hadn't come back. Steven hated crawling under the house.

Last summer he'd had to crawl under with some cans of antiflea spray, after mangy dogs set up shop in the under-house underworld. He'd worn a bandanna around his face but felt sick afterward. Once he had to crawl under when his dad was out of town to look for a leaking pipe. It was disgusting down there. Worms and roots and rotting wood. Some old paint cans. He put on his worst jeans and a ripped T-shirt and gritted his teeth.

"Here, Jesse!" he clicked and trilled. What was that old sound he used to do? "Kitty kitty kitty!" High, in a girl voice. After Jesse left, he'd gotten a turtle from his science teacher. Actually paid a dollar for it. The turtle, Joey, had a real personality. People did not realize this about turtles. They thought of them generically, not individually—the way people thought about guys whose jeans hung down off their butts. Bad. Joey was shy. He only liked Steven, not other people. He pulled his head in when other people came around.

Joey lived in a red dish tub of water in the yard, sunned on a brick, ran around the grass during the afternoons. Steven had fashioned a little staircase of bricks so Joey could go in and out of the tub on his own. He slept in the water. Steven fed him stinky ReptoMin pellets and sliced bananas and apples. Actually Joey had bitten him, too, while Steven scrubbed his shell a bit too vigorously, but he never told anyone—how embarrassing was that? The first night after the bite he worried—could there be some bizarre virus transmitted through turtle bites? He looked it up on the internet. Of course he had secretly cleaned the wound and applied antibiotic cream, but the internet said he should take antibiotics by mouth, too. No way. Then he'd have to tell someone. Pets were not always so easy.

"Kitty kitty kitty!" he trilled. A slight movement off to the right. There he was—pitiful growling Jesse, hiding behind one of the wooden posts that held the house up.

Steven started backing out from under the house. "Mom, I found him! Call Animal Control immediately! He still seems mad!"

Joey the turtle was hibernating right now. Steven suddenly missed him. At least he couldn't lunge or leap.

Jesse's tail thickened. He howled and showed his teeth again. "Enough of that, Buster," Steven hissed. "You ran away, we didn't!"

According to some sources, Salinger had suffered post-traumatic stress from his wartime experiences. Or maybe his reclusiveness was a decisive marketing strategy—if you disappear, people are more interested in your work. You become a legend while you're still alive. Crouching behind a stone wall, or the post under a house . . . people are kneeling down to find you.

There Is No Long Distance Now

"I hate my name," said Brad.

"Why?" asked Sophie. She was twelve and hadn't thought much about her name, except when kids called her Sofa which she didn't mind because she loved cuddling up on any couch.

"You are so *young!*"

He was standing at the kitchen counter mixing his bizarre daily breakfast potion of strange amino acid substances, protein powders, a tiny glass of juice, a half banana, and a handful of wheat germ. He was working on his *body*.

"How was the party?"

"Horrible. No, fun—in a bloodshot kind of way."

"Did you drink alcohol?"

He snorted. Soon she would be asking him which parts

of his girlfriend's beautiful body he had actually touched. And he would say, her hand, sweetheart, only her hand. The truth was, he had no girlfriend. Everyone was his girlfriend. This was his theory—float and drift. Be in love with everyone you see. The heart is a bucket without a lid. Maybe he read it in a play. But it seemed to work.

"I had one sip of wine."

"You did not."

"Maybe not."

"You better not. You are only seventeen."

"And what are you, a cop? Thank you for informing me. I still hate my name."

Sophie loved Brad so much. She loved to go anywhere with him and be identified as his little sister. He could open hard things. He had biceps. He told her important facts about the world, such as, There is really no long distance now, as there used to be in the old days, when it took a long time to find out what was happening in Ireland or Iraq or Saudi Arabia. Sophie had an e-pal in Saudi Arabia, a girl named Suheir who dreamed of being a pilot, in a country where her mom couldn't even drive a car.

In class, when asked to write about heroes, Sophie was the only one who wrote about her brother. Mike with the stupid buzz cut asked, "Are you in love with him?" and she said, "You are so weird." But she was, in a way. She wanted to be his protector, his bodyguard. She wanted to go to parties with him and hold up her hand against beer bottles which came within twenty feet of her brother. She had read about alcohol poisoning and it really worried her. Already she had joined the campaign against texting while driving. She wanted him safe.

One good thing she realized—he cared so much about his *body* he would surely not take drugs or do other abusive things to it. Quick-witted. That's what he was. She had to write a poem which used the letter *Q* six times, at the beginnings of lines, so she kept thinking of *q* words without even trying to. The assignment seemed in keeping with her teacher's love for Quirky assignments. Quiet, Quintessential, Queries, Quit. She was sure other people would use Queen, Queer, Quest.

"Why do you think he likes violent movies when he could be in *any* movie?" Brad often talked to himself when the blender was on.

"What? Who?"

"Brad Pitt. He could do anything he wants to do. But still he does stupid violent movies, too."

"He does?"

"I mean, *Benjamin Button* was worth his time, but some of these others?"

Sophie knew nothing about Brad Pitt. She knew about Miley Cyrus and Flight of the Conchords. She had watched most of the Flight segments three times already on HBO and

owned both seasons on DVD. Their parents thought the con-
tent a little "old" for her, but somehow Jemaine's and Bret's
New Zealand accents and goofy music softened things. Miley
was so versatile—singing, dancing, acting so funny, bouncing in
and out of scenes—Sophie just adored her. She would not have
minded to be named Miley but . . . suddenly she understood.

"Do you feel like people *compare* you to Brad Pitt?"

"Of course. Our likenesses are irresistible. He has a
dozen children and I'm seventeen."

"No, he doesn't!"

"What are you looking for? Q words. Sister, you are
Quaint."

Sophie sometimes couldn't tell what was a compliment
and what wasn't.

Brad continued, "Did you know Mom had some leci-
thin pills in the bathroom cabinet that expired in 1991?"

"Before I was born!"

"Before either of us were born!"

"That's quirky! And did you take one?"

"Guess what, I threw them out. And what about that
ancient shampoo bottle she keeps refilling from the bulk
barrel at the grocery, then hides in the back of the cabinet so
no one else will use it?"

"Yes. She said the bottle has sentimental value and it will
be the last bottle she ever uses. Her own style of recycling."

"Did Dad give it to her or what?"

"I don't know. It seems strange to be attached to a shampoo bottle."

Brad held out his tall blue glass and said, "Taste this!"

Sophie pinched her nose. "No way! It's so thick I would gag!"

"You'll love it! You'll have twice as much energy all day!"

Why did anyone want that much energy? Sophie felt fine. She liked everything, even her toothbrush, which was turquoise, a word which came from the Arabic language originally, as did *lime, jar, gazelle, cotton, mask, yoghurt, monsoon, oasis, mocha, algebra, average, giraffe, soda, adobe, crimson, sugar,* and *mummy*.

She had apologized to Suheir for the mean things some people at her school said about Muslims, and Suheir wrote back, "I am thinking about your letter. I don't know what to say. I know you do not feel that way."

Sophie asked Brad, "Do you think I shouldn't have brought it up? Did I hurt her feelings?"

He said, "It was a little rude. If she had *asked* you about it, that's one thing. But bringing it up out of nowhere would be like me telling you my friends call you Dorothy from *The Wizard of Oz*. Your retro hairdo and shiny red shoes."

My Boyfriend, John Mayer

Today my mom told me she wants to get married again. But she hasn't met the person yet. I'm not even sure if it will be a man or a woman. Wait, I said to her. Please wait. Wait till I move out and then you can do anything you like.

We were in the car at the corner by The Cove, that strange Laundromat/car wash/music joint/fish taco stand combined into one place, and I was thinking if that place were a person, it might have a diagnosis. My mom sighed. She said, Do you want a fish taco? I said, No, I want to wash all my clothes. Lately I've been thinking how some people start off on a path and just stay on it and other people jump from path to path trying to decide which one to keep going on. And basically when you are a teenager, that is your main business, to discover if you are on a path you want to be

on, or can stand being on, or if you are still jumping to find
another one. And the people who get into big trouble sometimes are the ones who fall into a crack or space or ditch
between the paths and just get stuck there.

For the first years of my life I thought everything was my
fault. Everyone in my family was some kind of wreckage—my
mom, my dad, even my grandpa with his gin bottles all lined
up on the kitchen table like bowling pins, and Uncle Lou.
Pretty self-centered, isn't it? How could a five-year-old kid
be responsible for so many people? What was the common
denominator? Who did they all know? Me. It had to be my
fault. Never dawned on me that they all knew each other, too.

When Mom was in a good mood, we had a blast, basically. We read about someone in the newspaper who was
growing tall native grasses out by Lake Medina, and she
said, Do you want to go see that? Yes, I said, and we hopped
in the car. That's why Dad left, basically. He could never
find us. He'd come home from work and we'd be down at
Port Aransas. Once we volunteered to work at the giant sea
turtles refuge and forgot to call home for a whole weekend.

But Mom's gloomier episodes, which sometimes lasted
a year or more, they were tough. That's when I started hiding out in my room, snipping up magazines, making collages
using a lot of eyes from *Vanity Fair* ads, those big painted
makeup eyes, gigantic Penélope Cruz–style. I'd sit there at

my desk with scissors and a glue stick and small cardboard rectangles to paste everything on and play John Mayer really loud and it was okay. It was comforting. I'd come out and show my creations to my mom, who was usually dozing in the big chair after work, the disgusting fat chair with a remote control device, which I have always refused to sit in, and she'd look at them without smiling and close her own eyes again. Maybe that's why I was so obsessed with eyes. I wanted them to stay open.

The day before Uncle Lou fell asleep on the train track, he came by our place and told my mom he was real, real afraid of growing old. So what's the alternative, Lou? she asked him. As far as I could tell he was already old, so I listened in with some interest. He said, Checking out, Sissy. That's the only alternative. And my mom, who was kinda down then, really popped up onto a higher rung when she heard that. She said, Lou, you stay for dinner. I'm going to make macaroni and cheese, the old-fashioned scratch way you like it, with real crumbs on top, and he didn't get excited at all. I'm starting to grate the cheese right now, Mom said. I noticed with some interest how a person who is down seems much improved when faced with someone who is more down than they are. It's all a matter of degrees. She said to me then, Why don't you show some of your collages to Uncle Lou, while I make dinner? This seemed highly far-fetched and not like something that was going to, you know, bring him up a notch, but I said, Sure thing, Mom, trying to act bright and normal as I always did when faced with people who were on the far side of regular, which was just about like every minute.

So we went into my room and Lou saw a poster of John Mayer and he said, Is that your boyfriend? I started laughing so hard and said, In my dreams. He said, Who is it really? And I played him maybe the wrong choice of song, about every little past frustration, which Lou certainly had a lot of, and also about the shadows in your head and all, but basically the song says, Step up, say it, open your heart, say it clearly, you know? So, was that bad? It even says it's better to talk too much than too little. Which I could certainly underscore. But, trust me, I thought about it later, the train tracks, that song running through Lou's head, what was he saying to us?

Um, I don't really know what I need right now.

I think I need a friend I never met before. Someone without any tangle of history that intersects with mine or my family's. So we could start over at some other spot, like a log at the beginning of a trail. I need a new log. And a new path. Like that thing I was saying. It's time to jump.

I think I need a long walk over some ground that isn't too rough, like Nebraska.

I wouldn't mind some big geese flying over and shouting and stuff.

Where We Come From

"A bully and a religious fanatic."

"A righteous banker and a flirt."

"An agoraphobic and a daydreamer."

"A shopping addict and a masochist."

"A worrywart and a beer drinker."

They were sitting around the lunch table describing their parents, the odd combinations of people who had made them, wellsprings of their DNA. Many of these jolly duets were now divorced, but still their parents nonetheless. They tried to outdo one another.

"A drug dealer and a spoiled brat."

"Your dad isn't a drug dealer!"

"Historically, yes."

No wonder they were a little strange themselves.

"I have not seen my father in four months." (Sharif, whose father taught in Cairo)

"I have never seen my father." (Juan Carlos)

"My mother says if she sees my father she'll kill him. That's really nice for us." (Tyrone)

Annie could never say, "My father is so sweet, I hope I die before he does." Because sometimes it seemed she was the only person with a sweet anyone.

Rick said his father had been under a car since the day he was born. His dad's brand of happiness: greasy wrenches, oily jeans. Rick said he was never going to get a driver's license. "I will work for public transit. To defy the family gene."

A daughter was supposed to have an extra dose of her father's mother's DNA in her. Annie had never known her father's mother—she'd died in a car accident before Annie was born. But Annie adored her father's aunt, a vibrant German Texan ranch woman who said, "I've turned into one of the little old ladies I used to make fun of."

"No, you didn't!"

"Yes, I did. I still make fun of them when I see them wearing checkered pink shirts with striped red skirts, or too much rouge. Don't you have eyes? I ask myself. You nutty old lady. Then I realize I'm older than they are and I'm wearing *gingham*."

Age was such a mystery. Some people felt old when they
were three. And some never seemed old. Annie's great-aunt
could drink a cup of coffee at eleven p.m., then go straight
to sleep. She was disturbed that no one "knew goats" anymore. Except 4-H kids. She said when she was little, living
out by San Angelo in the rocky country of great horizons,
people understood goats' needs and intentions; they knew
how to talk to them and listen, too.

"Spitzy, I think I'm okay," Annie said. "Not talking to
goats. I don't think I'm too lonely for them."

"You would be if you knew what you are missing."

Also, people had lost an essential skill before discover-
ing it. Spitzy was saddened that so many young people grew
up these days not knowing how to ride horses. A serious
omission. Rick said he would ride a horse if he had one.

"You all want to meet up at Spitzy's someday? She'd
cook us a big pot of stew or some chili and corn bread.
She'd love you!"

"No one loves me." (Tyrone)

"We all love you!" (Chorus at cafeteria lunch table)

Spitzy displayed a joie de vivre contagious beyond
belief. How could anyone be happy living in such a jum-
ble? Annie always wanted to help her great-aunt clean up.
But no, she was keeping those six old cracked dish drainers
just in case. Dusty horse blankets, empty plant containers,

half-burned Christmas candles, baskets, laces, mumbo jumbo of clutter tied together with a leaky garden hose. On the porch. That was just the porch.

Sometimes Annie asked her dad to drive her west to Kerrville so she could stay with Spitzy for the weekend. "I'm needing some rice pudding, Dad." Spitzy refused to come into the city anymore since there was so much traffic and all the downtown carriage horses were enslaved, made to wear fake floral wreaths on their heads to haul around honeymooners. Annie's dad always had to get back to the city for a meeting or a lunch. What was the adult fascination with lunches?

"When I grow up, I am *never* going to make lunch dates," Annie said to Spitzy. They were drinking lemonade with mint. "Not for weekdays, certainly not for weekends. It's been bad enough having to eat with all those same people at school every single day."

Spitzy said, "You'll miss them later, baby. Oh, how I miss my old friends! Even though they're all around here still. Somewhere. Or in nursing homes. Or dead. Sometimes I hear their voices come across a field clear as day."

"Clear as day?"

"Better than."

Most days weren't clear when you were in them. What kind of day did Spitzy remember?

"Sharp as broken glass. I wore a thick linen skirt, cream colored, with a few blotches on it, and a denim shirt, beat-up cowboy boots, and stood in that pasture you liked when you were little, with the bushy soft tall grass. The light was sinking, I could feel my breath inside my skin, traveling and flowing into every corner of me, and my mind so alive, fully aware of any little fly that sat on my wrist or breeze that passed by my head, and I looked out and said, Someday, when you're almost dead, remember this feeling, cold as water drunk with your head thrown back, remember it, that you were here in your boots in the grasses with the birds in the far trees, you were alive and young, so much was still coming, tragedies, history, presidents, lovers, cakes, even cakes were coming, the old-fashioned vanilla rich cakes that used to sink in the middle but what a delicious texture they had, real crumbs, hardly needed icing with a cake like that. We could go back in the house and try to make one. You want to?"

Annie stood up a little taller. A breeze brushed both of them.

Spitzy stared at her. Annie smiled. "That sounds good."

Tomorrow, Summer

"We were stooges. We were freshmen." Manny wished he had not brought it up. Especially today, when they were excited about graduating—he'd thrown a shadow into the room.

Mirage said, "Please tell me it is not true. I can't stand it."

Four years ago, they'd been loitering outside the cafeteria when, for whatever reason (she and Manny liked to linger and flirt), she'd impersonated their horrible biology teacher. Mirage rarely mocked people—even the girls painstakingly repairing their black nail polish in the bathroom. But the biology teacher had made fun of her name—"Do some people call you Illusion?"—and he was the dullest person on earth.

Mirage had mastered his low, crackly drawl. "Stoooooodents, re-mooooove all your exCESS beLONGings from the TOPS of your desks. No cell phones, all SYStems OFF. Prepare for classssssssssss. To-DAY! We will analyze the compoNENTS of . . . DUMB DUMB DUMB AND BOR-ING THINGS!" Then she gargled and coughed, raising her right hand to half-cover her mouth, as he always did, to the consternation of people sitting in the front row. Why did he emphasize certain syllables so strangely? Was he translating from nematode language even as he spoke?

There was almost no way to escape having Mr. Ray, unless you had an allergy to frogs. Tall and bald, with one of those protruding stomachs on an otherwise beanpole frame, he had, by the fourth day of class, succeeded in hyp-notizing even the most avid academics into a biological stu-por. Mirage said his first name was Ambien. Ambien Ray. Sounded like a fish.

Manny had laughed and said, "I think he has acid reflux. That hacking dry cough thing. Do you think he goes onto automatic pilot the minute the bell rings?"

Mirage had once, in class, answered Mr. Ray in his own cadence unconsciously. He asked, "Do I detect an insult?" which made everyone titter.

Amal, the Pakistani girl, helped her out that day. She interjected, "Mr. Ray, we were discussing the possibility of a visit to the botanical gardens, since they have that new frog pond and we could perhaps get a group tour . . . would you like me to check on it?" Mirage and Amal chatted more often after that. At the botanical gardens, they watched a Venus flytrap eat a fly together.

But Amal was nowhere nearby the day Mirage impersonated Mr. Ray and he came around the corner and stopped right in front of her and Manny. He stared into her eyes. He said, "Am I that bad?"

She froze. A sadness shaded his gaze. He said, "I know, I'm not the most animated guy on earth." He looked down, and up again. "Sorry about that," he said. Then he walked away. Manny said, "Ouch." Mirage covered her face with her hands.

The year rolled on. Mirage wrote an apology note to Mr. Ray and left it on his desk, but he never mentioned it. She worked hard on biology but felt awkward answering questions in class or even meeting his eyes. At the end of the year, her grade was a B. The next year when she and Manny were sophomores, Mr. Ray retired at Christmas, surprising the new crop of hypnotized biologists.

Then Manny had run into him at a grocery store a few months later. He was looking thinner and paler than usual.

"Mr. Ray!" Manny said. "How are you doing?" and Mr. Ray said, "Not so good, actually, I've had some challenges." After a long pause, he added, "They tell me I have about a month or two."

Manny said, "That's terrible!" He struggled for something else to say. Then, "Mr. Ray, we—miss you at school. You were—a really good teacher."

"No, I wasn't," he said. "I'll never forget your little friend—how well she played me. I guess I didn't have that stand-up gene that would have made me interesting. I just loved my—topic."

His obituary would say he had a brother in Rockport. That was it. There wasn't even a memorial mentioned.

And Manny had made the mistake of repeating the whole grocery conversation to Mirage, right now, today, because they were graduating and might not see each other again and he'd never brought it up before.

She looked as if he'd punched her. Her eyes filled with tears and spilled right over. "I hate myself."

"No, you don't. We all make mistakes. C'mon, forget about it! Geez, I should never have said anything."

She said, "He told you that and then he *died*."

"Well, trust me, you had nothing to do with his death. Change the subject. Think of summer! I am truly ready for summer, aren't you? I am looking forward to returning to my old apron and being charming to nasty people again."

Manny was a waiter at Joe's Crab Shack. He had the patter down.

Johnnie

Spitzy wasn't getting out of bed anymore. She stayed in bed as the sunlight filtered into her room and traveled silently up the wall, touching her bent photograph of Otto in a pasture and a faded yellow and green cross-stitch that said, simply, "HOME." She was leaving the dog food bag wide open so her dog Muscatine could have breakfast when he was ready, sticking his muzzle deep into the chow.

"Dad, it's bad," Annie said, after another weekend with her favorite great-aunt. "When you start letting your pet feed himself, that's a bad sign."

"Old age is a bad sign in general." Her dad sighed. "What can I do? She won't come into town and live with us. She won't allow anyone to be hired to help her. You have to go to school, so you can't live out there all the time. Who's feeding her, did she tell you?"

"Some lady named Rosie from down the street comes by every day with a plate lunch from the church. Then Spitzy parcels it out to become three meals. I think she saves the bun for next day's breakfast. I made some noodles for her, and some blueberry crumble."

"And her bathroom business?"

"She gets up sometimes. For that only. But very, very slowly. Then she goes straight back. I tried to give her a little bath in bed. She won't step over the edge of the tub any-more—she says she won't be able to get back out."

Annie paused. She didn't know whether to tell him or not.

So she blurted it. "And there was a man in bed with her a few days ago, when Rosie went by. Rosie told me."

"*What?*"

"A youngish man, not an old one. He was lying on top of the covers next to her with his clothes on. They weren't doing anything. But Spitzy was asleep and he was awake."

"This is the worst thing I ever heard."

"No, it's not. But it's really weird, that's for sure."

"It's insane. He could rob her blind."

"What does she have?"

"What?"

"What could he rob?"

After he'd caught his breath, Annie's dad asked, "Did Rosie recognize him?"

"No."

Her dad shook his head. "Spitzy is a tough cookie."

"She's proud of it. She doesn't like pity."

Her dad sighed again. He always seemed so tired when anything about his family came up. Annie figured his tiredness had most to do with his long-dead dad, Spitzy's brother, but they didn't mention it. Some people you couldn't make happy, no matter what you did. And you certainly couldn't make them happy after they were gone.

Annie went to school that day wondering about the man in the bed. Maybe he was just a homeless dude Spitzy took pity on. One of her long-lost handymen. Maybe he was just out of jail, en route to work on a ranch at Big Spring—Spitzy wouldn't fear such a person. She'd figure he'd been rehabilitated, his good qualities polished by lockup—a hardworking cowboy again. Once she'd taken in two runaway girls from Killeen and talked them into phoning home, then bought them bus tickets back.

Annie called Spitzy after school. She answered on the sixth ring. "Spitzy, who was the guy in bed with you a few days ago when Rosie brought you lunch?"

"My boyfriend."

When Annie said, "Come on!" Spitzy said, "Do I bug you about yours?" But Annie didn't even have one.

Annie asked her father if she could transfer to Kerrville High School so she could live with Spitzy and watch over her, for the spring semester of junior year only. She'd be back in time for senior year. If she were there to take care of her auntie, she'd gain something more precious than another dull semester in the company of her classmates. And by summer, or fall, Spitzy would be better, or worse, and they could reevaluate. The only problem was—the log cabin didn't have two bedrooms. It was hard to imagine sleeping in the same room with Spitzy—a second bed wouldn't fit. Maybe Annie could sleep on the piled-high daybed in the living room. She'd clean it off and find forty treasures. And wouldn't it be somehow exotic to try out another high school for one semester only?

So she was stunned when her dad said, "I don't want you to go. What if that guy comes back? It's too loose up there. I don't think she even has locks. I can't look after you."

Annie laughed out loud. "Look after me?" She felt insulted. Half the time she felt she was looking out for him—picking up his socks, making him high-protein smoothies for breakfast.

"Let's think about this," her dad said. "There's still time before Christmas break. Let's talk about it after we think about it."

But by Christmas Spitzy had started seeing ghosts in the fireplace and had tried to feed them bread and salt from her church tray.

Annie spent weekends with Spitzy as before but had a hard time understanding things she said—there were so many breaks in stories, jumbled images. Spitzy asked for a bedpan. Something had changed.

Dad said they needed to check her into a rehab facility in Kerrville to get her walking again. Spitzy said she was finished with walking and rejected medical attention. Two of her friends had died from lethal drug combinations prescribed by doctors and she wanted no doctors.

On the Friday before New Year's, Rosie found her curled up in bed as if she were just sleeping, but she didn't wake up—it was fish day, too. The church meal she liked best, and now she wouldn't get to eat it. She'd left a piece of paper on the table, "For Johnnie" with a heart drawn beside the words, nothing for Rosie or Annie or Annie's father, and no further information.

Freshen Up

The man with a frizzy gray braid unzipped his stained brown jacket and pitched it into the washing machine. Unbuttoned his dusky green checkered shirt, rolled it into a ball, threw it in, too. Pulled off an orange short-sleeved T-shirt and a raggedy sleeveless white undershirt. Threw it all in. An open hand, like the Hand of Fatima, was tattooed on his back. Rainey watched from behind, transfixed. Four layers. You never really knew how many layers people had.

Leo stood next to her, also staring. They'd been folding towels like the married couple they would someday be when the man started stripping.

"Wow," Leo mouthed.

Then the pants. He unzipped his blue jeans and pulled them off. He wore boxer shorts with yellow cartoon ducks printed on them. Leo shook his head, finger to lips. Rainey imagined him saying, Stop there, stop there. And the man did stop. He bent over in his unexpectedly cheery boxer shorts, pulled wads of dirty laundry from a canvas bag at his feet—a towel, a blue sheet—and pitched it all in. Frenzy of movements, how satisfying to put things where they needed to go.

The man spun around, caught them looking, didn't acknowledge them, unfolded a black T-shirt from a short pile on the table and pulled it over his head. Tugged on another pair of jeans. No layers this time. Whipped around, slid a handful of quarters into the slot, dumped in some powdered soap from a bag, and pressed the button. The machine started whirling. Then he plucked a bag of Kettle potato chips from the top of the machine, ripped it open, and popped a handful into his mouth. All planned out. Thirty minutes wash, comin' right up. He walked over to the rack by the door, grabbed the free newspaper, and turned to the Love Wanted classifieds. Rainey poked Leo. "The one part I always skip," she said.

He nodded, whispering, "You're a lucky girl."

Later, in the parking lot, Leo said, "So there's number one. And we got a surprise, some guy freshening up right in the building."

Rainey and Leo had a new plan. Every weekend

they'd do three things they'd never done before. See what they could see. The clothes dryer was broken at Rainey's house. Her mom had asked if there was any chance she might haul the basket of wet laundry to a Laundromat. Sure! Rainey said. Number one. She'd never gone to a Laundromat with Leo.

Number two, the Damaged Discount Food Store in Leo's neighborhood. He'd passed it forever and never stepped inside. Dented cans. Unpopular brands. Anyone uncertain about the nation's economy had only to glance at the mobbed parking lot. They were glad they had walked. Women pushed rickety carts piled high with frozen French fries and mysterious frozen lumps of . . . meat? Not everything was damaged and some things seemed much more discounted than others. German foods abounded—why? How had all these wayward packages of spaetzle and plump jars of sauerkraut ended up in the discount bins? They wandered past thank you cards—a dying breed—and French shampoo for oily hair. Leo purchased a can of treacle pudding from England. Rainey selected an attractive jar of pesto sauce and a set of cards that said "Thanks a Million." When had the word "million" become so popular? It seemed strange to see it in a discount store.

The man who ran the store stepped right into their path with a wooden box of smoked wild salmon in his hands. He said, "This is only six bucks. I can tell you'd like it." Rainey and Leo stared at each other. Smoked salmon was one of their favorite foods. Both of them. How had he known? And what was it doing here? The box wasn't battered.

"Gee, thanks, we'll take it," said Leo. "And what's your favorite thing?"

"Smoked salmon," the man said.

Later, spreading small bits of tasty salmon onto whole-wheat crackers with goat cheese, marveling at food tasting so good, they wondered—how had that guy zeroed in on them in the store? Did he walk up to other people and say, "Here, corn nuts, just what you love." Was he a psychic grocer? Did they look like exiled Alaskans?

Number three, the serious one. Their outings couldn't all be easy. Visits to the military hospital would be ongoing, if they could stand it, and the hospital let them continue to come. They weren't paying homage, either. Trying to understand, was more like it.

Rainey hated killing, and weapons, and war so much, she had negative feelings when she saw soldiers. Maybe meeting some would help. They'd made an appointment.

The volunteer coordinator sent Leo into a ward to sort mail and newspapers.

Rainey was handed a stack of magazines and entered the room of a freckled soldier with one arm and one leg gone, and a black eye patch. She paused, then said shyly, "Hi, Nick."

He squinted. "Hey you. Little gal. Are you the reader?"

She laughed. "How do you feel about someone reading to you?"

"Great," he said. "Especially if she's cute. What about *National Geographic*, maybe? Something about the sea?"

As she fanned pages awkwardly, he blurted, "It was the worst mistake of my life to go to war." Then he started crying. Just like that.

Would she get kicked out? He talked for fifteen minutes. She cried, too.

"Thank you for being so honest," she said. "I'm very sorry about what happened to you."

"So read about fish," he said. "The big fish that eat littler ones like it's normal."

Will You Hold My Bullet, Please?

In those days there were many things we did not want.

Our father drove us to Mexico because the dentist was cheaper.

We never said the word "poor." *How much did the gas cost, Dad?* Gas was cheap then.

There were no interesting towns between San Antonio and Nuevo Laredo, only scrub brush and cactus, then the irritating wait at the border.

So I was happy on our second visit when the Mexican dentist tripped on a mat, stabbing me in the knee with a metal pick.

The wound bled generously. Our father would never take us there again.

He found an affordable dentist in a San Antonio building called Collins Garden. Yesterday I saw it being smashed
by a wrecking ball—dusty mountain of concrete, smoked
glass simmering in heat. Good-bye, Monopoly delusions. . . .

Lyman, the new dentist, appeared to have little interest in
dentistry.

While "cleaning our teeth" with bleaching potion (no
brushing, flossing, or scraping), he spoke of Mexican music,
land deals in south Texas, the pleasures of rural living. Later
we visited Lyman at his home, a rundown stucco hacienda in
a field of scrub brush and cactus. We waited five hours for a
fish to be grilled in a pit. Our father began calling him "My
friend!" and went to lunch with him. Lyman wanted us all
to call him by his first name, which made me wonder if he
was really a dentist.

My teeth did not feel clean.

Soon our father bought land from Lyman. Though we never
seemed to have any extra money, apparently Dad and the
dentist made some sort of deal and the land was going to
become more valuable in six months, which of course it
never did.

The land was tucked away on a rutted road near the
Polish settlement of Panna Maria. For two months we spent

time looking for it. My father carried a map drawn on a napkin from a Mexican café where he and Lyman had sealed the deal.

It was the ugliest land ever. Even the mesquites were twisted—the shade from their gnarled branches felt ominous. Holes where snakes lived, mysterious ditches, heaps of rotten wood. Our father stared at us. "Someday this will all be yours."

One evening he took a deep breath. "I have bad news. Our friend Lyman has been arrested."

"What?"

"A week ago. I just heard about it. He wants me to visit him at the jail."

"For selling ugly land or for being a bad dentist? For what, Dad?"

"Cocaine."

"Cocaine?" I had never heard my father say the word before. It did not seem right in his vocabulary—like *quesadilla* or *toreador*. "What was he doing with it? Using or selling it?"

"Perhaps being a repository—storing it for others. He may not have known what he had."

"Sure, that sounds likely."

I had never smoked pot or taken an aspirin. Cocaine

seemed like a ticket to the underworld for all I knew. My dad asked me to go to the jail with him. "Why, Dad? I don't *like* Lyman. I'm sure he has no desire to see me."

"Well, do it for me. I need your support."

So we drove to the jail. Lyman could only have one visitor at a time.

"I'll just wait on the sidewalk, Dad. Or take a walk." Prisoners shouted through the grillwork. "Baby, bring me a burger!"

I could not imagine Lyman cooped up in such an environment. Despite his eccentricities, he was an optimist with geraniums growing in clay pots.

My father paused. He wore his blue *guayabera* shirt, tucked pockets and pearly buttons. "Honey, I need you to hold this for me while I go in. I'm shocked, really. I just reached for my ID at the security desk. Glad they didn't notice. . . ."

My father handed me a bullet. He shrugged. "I'm not sure what this is."

"Dad? Are you serious? You want me to sit in front of the jail, a raggedy teenager, *holding a bullet*? Dad, why do you *have* a bullet? Do you have a gun?"

"Not on me," he said.

"But you have one?"

It stunned me that my gentle father, who once cried

when he caught a mouse in a mousetrap ("I didn't realize it would *kill them*"), could think of owning one. What was he doing with it?

Wild dogs. Those nuts who phoned Mom to say they had Dad tied up. Burglars. He never mentioned what surely was the real reason he owned a gun—he got a good deal on one. Possibly Lyman had sold it to him. Maybe it was the bonus for owning that hideous land. One day you would wake up and need to commit suicide. I said, "Dad, this is nuts."

He shrugged again, sheepish. He knew something was a little "off" in the scene. And I strode down the block with a bullet in my pocket, through the baked streets of San Antonio summer, past the twenty-four-hour bail office, the sagging Cactus Hotel sign, the store for checkered western wear, the greasy Cadillac Bar. Not yet the bearer of a driver's license, I felt the weight of undesirable things I would be forced to carry as an adult—tax receipts, mortgages, other people's artillery accessories, etc. I weighed a thousand pounds. Lyman would be in jail a long time, then get out and die. The land he had sold us would become a smudge in a history of shaky transactions. My father would die. No gun of any kind would be found among his pitiful possessions at the time of his death. Even the building called Collins

Garden would be crushed into rubble decades later during a sudden rainstorm, as diners at La Fonda up the block raced from patio tables into the restaurant proper, holding menus over their heads against the surprise.